DOWN ON HER Knees
A DARE ME NOVEL

DOWN ON HER Knees

A DARE ME NOVEL

USA TODAY BESTSELLING AUTHOR
CHRISTINE BELL

This book is a work of fiction. Names, characters, places, and incidents are the product of the author's imagination or are used fictitiously. Any resemblance to actual events, locales, or persons, living or dead, is coincidental.

Copyright © 2014 by Christine Bell. All rights reserved, including the right to reproduce, distribute, or transmit in any form or by any means. For information regarding subsidiary rights, please contact the Publisher.

Entangled Publishing, LLC
644 Shrewsbury Commons Ave
STE 181
Shrewsbury, PA 17361
rights@entangledpublishing.com

Brazen is an imprint of Entangled Publishing, LLC.

Edited by Kerri-Leigh Grady and Allison Blissard
Cover design by LJ Anderson/Mayhem Cover Creations
Cover photography by VitalikRadko/Deposit Photos

Manufactured in the United States of America

First Edition February 2014

ENTANGLED
BRAZEN

To the readers of the Dare Me series who wanted Rafe and Courtney's story, this one's for you!

Chapter One

Courtney DeLollis huddled in the corner of the grandly appointed reception tent, peering through the leaves of a giant ficus, hoping the foliage would shield her from sight. If she played her cards right, maybe she'd get through the evening in the background, present and accounted for, but not having to engage with anyone. And by anyone, she meant—

"The sleek puma sits back on her haunches, waiting for her prey to stop sniffing the air, all the while scouring the group for the weakest link."

The low male voice in her ear made her tense until it was followed by a chuckle she knew well. She resisted the urge to slump with relief and turned to face Galen Thomas.

"Hey there, handsome. You guys looked great out there," she said.

Wasn't that the truth. Galen and his wife of less than two hours, Lacey, both looked gorgeous. The groom in his gray tux, his bride in her white dress with a blue sash. On a beautiful summer evening by the lake under a pristine white canopy surrounded by family and friends, their first dance had been pure magic. Someday, a long time from now, Courtney was going to find a man who looked at her the way they looked at each other.

Yep. A verrrry long time from now.

"You look pretty great yourself," Galen said and motioned to her dress. Even while he said it, though, he was scanning the canopied area for his bride. "Too nice to be hiding behind the potted plants. My wife has been trying to find you."

Shit. She'd hoped to fly under the radar. "Well, here I am," she said, waggling her fingers jazz-style. At his deadpan stare, she dropped her arms back to her side. "Fine. I'll be right out. I had to escape your Uncle Milton." Not the truth, but believable enough. The man was a talker. "He was yapping my ear off. It's fine now, though. He seems to have located the bar."

Galen laughed and nodded. "Okay, but don't go wandering off again. Lacey's worried because you don't know that many people here. You know how she gets. Plus the bridal party needs to be on call for pictures and then the throwing of the bouquet."

"Sure thing," she reassured him brightly. His astute gaze held hers for a beat too long, and he seemed ready to question her further but a female voice called to him.

"Did you find her?"

"She's right here," he yelled back to his wife, moving his hulking form to the side to offer visual confirmation. Lacey waved, and the tall man standing next to her followed suit.

Rafe Davenport.

Courtney's mouth went dry and a shiver ran through her. Six feet or better of lean muscle, he looked like he could have led the Trojans into battle if he had to. She had gotten to see him in his uniform a few months back when they'd all gone out for drinks to celebrate his commendation after he helped rescue a little girl lost in the woods. In his police blues, he was pure fantasy. In the tux, he gave James Bond a run for his money.

He leveled her with a mocking smile, as if he knew full well she was avoiding him, and she barely resisted the urge to flip him the bird. God, did he bring out the brat in her.

Besides, it wasn't like she was *hiding* from him, so much. She just wasn't in the mood to lock horns with him today, and staying out of sight was more foolproof than relying on her self-discipline. It seemed like whenever they were around each other, they got into some sort of beef that left her irritated, frustrated and way too aware of her body.

Apparently, he either didn't feel the same way or enjoyed the sensation, because he dipped his head to say something to Lacey and then made his way purposefully toward Courtney's foliage camouflage, long legs eating up the dance floor between them.

Talk about your puma. His focus was laser-like, and it took all her strength to stand her ground. So what. He was going to come over, break her balls, they'd do their little verbal sparring, and then he'd walk away. This wouldn't be the first time, and it wouldn't be the last. She needed to get better at managing him, was all. She loved her new group of friends, and he was part of the package, so the sooner she learned to deal with him, the better.

Straightening her shoulders, she tipped her head up to face him as Galen moved off to meet up with his wife.

"Hello, Courtney." Rafe's silky voice held a laugh right beneath the surface that had every muscle in her body tensing. She tried to calm the pounding of her heart as she offered a fake smile.

"Hey, Rafe." *That's it, Court. Keep it casual-like.* Only those eyes, black as pitch, sexy as sin, seemed to see right through her, and her smile wavered. *Say something else.*

"What can I do for you?" As soon as the words slipped from her lips, she wished for them back. Why did everything she said around him come off like it was sexual?

His already-hot gaze went hotter and he made a soft *snick*ing sound with his mouth. Chills broke out over her as he leaned in closer. Instinctively, she backed up, until the still-sun-warmed metal of the canopy post pressed against her spine.

"I think you know me better than to ask a question like that," he said softly.

The thing was, she didn't. Not really. They'd hung out as a group a lot, but the two of them had been like oil and vinegar. They'd mingle for a short while when forced, but that was about it. Something about him put her perpetually on edge. She'd managed to keep her wary distance until the night of Lacey's bachelorette party, when she'd found out he was some sort of bedroom dom. Which, while none of her business, hadn't been far from her thoughts ever since.

Her mistake had been calling him on it.

She pushed back the thought and took a sip of her wine to gather her wits before responding. "That's charming. Someone asks a simple question and you automatically make it into some BDSM thing. Why don't you scope the room for someone to handcuff to something?" she asked. "I'm a little busy right now."

He glanced down at the ficus she was clinging to with her free hand and shrugged. "Your date looks like a real bore. I'm just trying to liven things up a little. And for the record, I didn't mention anything about BDSM. You know, for someone who thinks it's abusive, you sure do bring it up a lot."

Only because he goaded her into it. *After you goaded him first,* her subconscious added helpfully. Okay, so maybe calling it "abusive" had been a stretch, but she'd been desperate. Willing to say anything at that point if it helped her throw up a roadblock between them before she did something stupid. What she hadn't realized was that he'd view her little red herring as bait. In her attempt to keep distance between them, she'd unwittingly opened Pandora's box and had no clue how to close it again.

Better to stay on the defensive until this thing ran its course or he got bored of messing with her. "Don't act like the victim here, Detective." She straightened, set her glass on a nearby side table, and laid a hand on his rock-hard chest to push him back a step. "You might be used to intimidating witnesses on the job, but I'm not a perp and I'm sure as hell not your sub. You've been yanking my chain about this for two weeks and I'm about sick of it."

"See, there you go again, talking about yanking and chains. It's stuck in your head now, isn't it?" He covered the hand she hadn't realized was still on his chest—gripping a handful of tuxedo—and squeezed. "It's okay to admit you're curious. Curiosity may have killed the *cat,* but if you give me ten minutes, I promise you'll walk away with a very satisfied—"

She released him and slapped her hands over her ears with a squeal. "Oh my God, you're seriously the most crass, rude, unbearable—"

In spite of her muffled hearing, there was no mistaking his laughter. He tugged at her wrists, devilment dancing in his eyes. "I was going to say 'smile on your face.' God, woman, what did you think I was going to say?"

Her cheeks burned, and she jerked her arms away from his grasp. "Nothing. Forget it."

This was why she couldn't be around him. He was too smooth for her, and as much as his cockiness irritated her, she also couldn't deny the lure. The naughty pull low in her belly that made her want to run and lean closer at the same time.

When had she last felt that way about a man?

Probably never.

But after her relationship with Wes, a guy like Rafe was the worst possible kind to wrestle with. Her ex had obliterated her confidence, taken over her life, and controlled her like a marionette, and she'd let it happen. Until she could learn to trust herself again, she sure as hell couldn't trust someone else. And when she did decide to get out there on the dating scene? It would be with a nice, mellow guy who let her call the shots. A tough-as-nails cop by day and bedroom dom by night was exactly what the doctor hadn't ordered.

Even as her gut seconded that notion, her thoughts went reeling back to the first time Rafe had offered her ten minutes of his undivided attention. The exchange was as fresh in her mind as if it had happened yesterday.

There he'd been, large as life, in the middle of the bar taking up way more than his fair share of the room, looking confident, sexy, and in control. She didn't know what happened. It was like the words had tumbled out of her.

"Expecting a woman to submit in bed is wrong, you know."

Even as she spoke, a vision of being draped over his lap, awaiting her punishment, filled her head. It was both terrifying and exciting, which only annoyed her more. Warning bells blared, reminding her that his sex life was none of her business, but her tipsy brain silenced the alarms and urged her on.

"Don't you worry that doing things to a woman when she's helpless and fantasizing about hurting her is a gateway to abuse? I have to wonder if it starts with a spanking in a bedroom and leads to a beating out of one."

Rafe seemed to consider her words but then shook his head. "Nope. You can wonder all you want, but if I deliver pain, it's only to intensify the pleasure later. I would never harm a woman, and I spend a lot of my workday hunting down men who do."

He pushed back his chair and stood. "Now, if you're through grilling me about my sexual practices, which you have no understanding or knowledge of, then I'm going to get myself a drink. Unless what you're really asking for is a lesson? In which case"—he glanced at his watch and then locked gazes with her—"you can pick up that hood and those cuffs"—he jerked his head toward the bachelorette party props—"and I'd be glad to take you outside in the alley and give you the best ten minutes of your life."

She stuttered and her whole body went white-hot, but she managed a tight smile and a damned good response. "As tempting as that is, if ten minutes is all you've got in you, I think I'll pass."

His responding grin was positively lethal. He leaned in close, the delicious scent of his aftershave battering her already-overloaded senses. His gaze traveled down the line of her neck, trailing over her breasts, where her nipples betrayed her, tightening. "Ten minutes isn't all I've got." Nostrils flaring as if he could sense her want, he bent low until his face was level with hers. "Ten minutes is all you could handle."

The repetitive clink of spoons on crystal dragged her back to the present and she cleared her throat, ignoring the tightening of her nipples beneath the thin chiffon dress. "Like I said, forget it."

"That's the problem." Rafe's voice sounded pained, raspy as he cut an exasperated hand through the air, and all signs of humor fled from his handsome face. "I want to forget it. I've tried to forget it. But fuck if I can. See, ever since that night, I'm in a bad way." He eyed her from head to toe, keen gaze taking in the arms crossed tightly over her chest. "And you don't seem to be any better off. You're all wound up. I'm all wound up. The perfect solution is to spend some time together and burn off this sexual tension."

He tucked a loose strand of hair back into the knot on the top of her head in a way that made her insides go to mush. Even with all the innuendo and teasing, she'd never really considered that he wanted her for real. She'd thought it was nothing more than a game to him. A way to make her pay, albeit in a playful way, for her digs about his sex life.

This wasn't that.

Her hands went from damp with sweat to icy cold in a flash at the realization. He was dead serious this time, and her already-overwrought nerves went haywire. This was *Black Hawk Down* emergency, worst-case-scenario-type serious. She could barely fight her attraction to him when he hadn't been trying. If he turned his full, unadulterated attention on her? She was dead in the water.

"No. Uh-uh. Not gonna happen," she said with a firm shake of her head that probably would've had a lot more oomph if her voice wasn't trembling. "Maybe I haven't been clear enough. I'm not in the market for a boyfriend, and—"

"Whoa." He stepped back like she'd tossed a vial full of acid at him. If she hadn't been such a wreck, she would have laughed. "Nobody said anything about a boyfriend. We're on the same page there."

"We are?" she asked, unable to stop herself from asking in spite of her ludicrously stinging pride.

"Yup." His posture relaxed some and he leaned back on his heels. "That's why we'd work perfectly together. I can show you how good giving up control in the bedroom can be, and you can help me get past this preoccupation I seem to have with you lately. When we're through, you walk away enlightened, and I…"

…*just walk away*, she finished for him silently when he trailed off.

She silenced the devil on her shoulder insisting that he'd

outlined the perfect solution to more than one problem and did what she did best.

Super-denial lockdown mode engaged.

She steeled herself and gave him a cool stare. "I'm sorry I gave you the wrong impression, Rafe. But I'm just"—she managed a nonchalant shrug even though she'd never felt more chalant—"not interested."

She tossed her head back and shouldered past him, his laughter following her across the room. It wasn't until she stood next to Cat and Lacey on the dance floor that she recognized the song pouring from the speakers around her.

"The Chicken Dance."

Lovely.

• • •

It was official. This woman was driving him batshit crazy. He watched from his perch at the bar while she danced with her friends and tried her damnedest to ignore him. Too bad she was terrible at it. Not the dancing. The dancing was good. His dick twitched in agreement as she shimmied back and forth, her hips mesmerizing him for a second before he refocused.

Nope, the part she sucked at was ignoring him. The veiled glances from beneath her lashes. The way her pupils dilated when she looked at him. The pulse in her neck beating wildly.

Not interested, his ass. But the offer had been made and declined. Time to move along.

"All the single ladies, head on over to the center of the floor for me, would you?" the DJ called, snagging Rafe's attention.

He took a sip from his glass of scotch and glanced at his watch. Another hour or so, a couple more corny traditions, and he could make a graceful exit. It probably wasn't too late to find a woman willing to play tonight. It had been weeks since he'd done a scene, and he was feeling the drought now.

He ran through a mental list of possible partners until he found himself distracted again by the woman in peach chiffon being dragged into a line by a group of laughing women.

He didn't look away until a shadow fell over the smooth lacquered bar. Galen Thomas stood over him, curiosity knitting his brows.

"What's going on with you two?"

He considered playing dumb, but they'd been friends for too long. Galen would get it out of him one way or another. "Hell if I know."

Galen snorted out a laugh. "That's a first. The guy with all the answers doesn't know. Are you actually digging her, or is this some tugging-braids-in-the-school-yard type of shit? Because I haven't seen you look at a woman like that since—"

After having boxed together before Galen went pro, the serious look on his face warned Rafe that it was about to get real, and he cut in, deflecting the blow neatly. Because hearing her name still hurt, even now.

"Nope." He took a long pull from his glass and set it down with a clink. "Courtney is sexy, and she's a challenge, but that's it. There's no love match here, so get it out of your head."

Galen had the audacity to look confused. "What do you mean? All I did was ask a simple question."

"I know that you and your pretty new wife are plotting to end my days of debauchery so I can follow you down the rabbit hole to wedded bliss, but that's not my bag, man. You done good, Lacey is a keeper, but that life's not for me."

Galen studied him like he was a creature under a microscope, and he braced himself for the second round. "Look, it's been five years now, man. Maybe it's time—"

Rafe cut him short again, anger making his voice tight. "I'm willing to bet you can still take me in the ring, but if you keep bringing Monica up, you and me are going to have a problem."

The words lay between them like a live wire, and despite the guilt that followed right on their heels, he refused to take them back. Not much was sacred to him, but this one thing? Not open for discussion, end of story, period.

Galen's gaze went flat, and for a second Rafe wondered if he was going to ignore his warning and push again. To his everlasting relief, his friend backed off with a curt nod instead.

"Got it."

Twelve years of friendship was long enough for Rafe to know that they were cool. At least, they would be as soon as the head of steam he'd built between them had burned off. Right now, though, the silence felt heavy. He was just about to break it with some clumsy attempt at small talk when the space around them reverberated with shouts of encouragement.

"Get ready, Lacey!"

The DJ counted down. "Five, four, three, two…"

They both watched as the bride pitched the bouquet over her shoulder, directly toward her maid of honor, Cat. She lunged for it, but suddenly began to pinwheel, arms flapping as she slipped on a cloth napkin. She landed in a laughing heap on the floor even as the bouquet headed like a missile at its new, unwitting target.

"Shit!" Courtney squeaked, lifting a hand up and barely plucking it out of the air in time to avoid it smacking her dead in the face.

"Damn," Cat grumbled, pushing herself to her feet to playfully glare at a stunned Courtney. "Looks like you're the next one getting married."

"Are you okay?" Lacey asked as the onlookers crowded around to make sure Cat was all right.

"I'm fine." She blew a copper-colored curl from her eye. "But this guy's in a load of trouble if he's going to wait until after she gets married to make an honest woman of me." She jerked a thumb at Shane, her live-in fiancé and another of Rafe's longtime buddies.

"Not to worry, love. It's an old wives' tale," he reassured her with a wink. "I'll take you whenever you'll have me."

Rafe strode over, attention on Courtney, who stood stock-still, hazel eyes wide with shock. "Did you get hit?" he asked, leaning closer to scan her face for injury.

"N-no. I'm fine." She stepped away, cheeks pink. "Let's keep it moving," she called to the crowd, her voice shrill. "Nothing to see here."

"You heard the young lady," the DJ crowed. "We're ready to rock and roll, so come on, let's get ready for the garter."

Rafe gave her one last glance, to see that she was all right. In spite of her reassurance, she still looked panicked, which didn't make sense. Surely she didn't believe in that antiquated mumbo jumbo about being the next one down the aisle?

He was still deep in thought, trying to solve the mystery behind Courtney's discomfort, as the festivities continued, with Galen making quick work of his bride's garter.

With everyone focused on the dance floor, maybe he didn't even need to stick it out the hour. Maybe he could sneak away—

"Where are you going?" Galen said, stopping him in his tracks.

"Jesus, you're fast."

"Right. Now answer the question."

He glanced out the tent and up the pathway with a regretful sigh, knowing he'd missed his window. "I was going to head out."

"No way." Galen planted his body in front of Rafe and gave him a grim smile. "You're in the wedding party, you can't leave. Get out there before you hurt my wife's feelings."

That was a low blow, but coupled with his guilt over being shitty to his buddy earlier, it worked. "Roger that." Rafe made his way to the line of men Galen was gesturing to, cursing under his breath all the while. Clearly another stupid tradition that he was glad he'd never have to go through again after today.

"Back up, assholes." A young guy with a dirty-blond buzz cut cracked his knuckles and hunkered down into what Rafe instantly recognized as a fighting stance. "Someone is about to get their hand up that chick's skirt, and it's gonna be me."

A couple of the other men laughed, most didn't, and Rafe's blood went hot.

"What the fuck are you talking about?" he growled at the frat boy, running through all the reasons he shouldn't knock that leering grin off his face with one clean uppercut.

"Where are you from, dude, Mars?" Blondie frowned. "Whoever catches the garter gets to put it on that girl."

Rafe hesitated. He didn't have any siblings and most of his friends were single, so he'd only been to one other wedding in his life and that one was in Texas, years ago with Monica. Still, surely he would've remembered that tradition? Before he could grill the guy further, Shane shouldered his way into the pack and confirmed the situation.

"Yeah. It's pretty standard, man."

Which explained Courtney's panic, and why she was strangling the bouquet in her white-knuckled hands. She was probably dreading the possibility of him catching the garter.

"Get your game face on," Shane urged in a low voice, clapping Rafe on the shoulder, hard. "I don't want to be here if this asshole next to me gets the garter. No matter what happens, remember, you're an officer of the law. Keep it legal."

Rafe nodded, but his focus was solely on Galen's hand as

he turned his back to the group and prepared to throw the tiny blue scrap of silk. Courtney might not want him up her dress, but there was no way in hell he was letting Frat Boy take advantage of her in the way he so clearly intended to.

When the garter came his way, the anger had drained away, leaving behind laser-like focus. And when Frat Boy checked him hard in the side, he checked him even harder back, sending the kid stumbling as his own fingers closed over the prize.

Even over the cheers of the guests, he heard Courtney's gasp and met her gaze, his tunnel vision expanding to include her. She sat on a chair in the middle of the dance floor, eyes wide as he walked toward her, unable to squash the rush of adrenaline pounding through him. He might make her nervous, but at least that other guy wasn't going to put his hands on her. If she knew what the bastard's intentions had been, she might actually be grateful right now.

And what about your intentions? his conscience whispered.

So maybe they hadn't always been pure, he conceded, but this time, he had only done what he'd done to protect her. He stopped in front of her chair and tipped his head at her.

"Ready for me?"

It wasn't supposed to come out like that. All low and growly. But his pulse was still jacked over the near-brawl, and looking down at her now and realizing what he had to do was only making it pound harder.

"Do your worst," she murmured, lifting her head dramatically, like she was at the gallows and he was her executioner.

His worst? Rafe let loose a rusty chuckle. Fuck, if she only knew how bad his worst could be, she'd already be up and running. Although he'd done his best, his worst, and everything in between to her a hundred times in his dreams.

The only thing that kept him in check was the realization that she had no clue what she was asking for. Because to a guy like him? That kind of declaration was an invitation. And in that way, a good bedroom dom was like a vampire.

An invitation was all he needed.

Not this time.

She'd made her position clear earlier, whether she meant what she'd said or not. He had to play nice.

He lowered himself to the floor, reluctantly slid off her strappy, fuck-me sandal and set it down next to him. She had a thing for shoes. Nearly every time he saw her, unless it was right after her shift at the hospital, she was in heels. Heels he couldn't help but imagine locked around his neck while she rode his tongue.

Jesus, he was no better than Frat Boy.

Except she wasn't looking at Frat Boy like he was a fat, forbidden slice of chocolate cake. She wouldn't admit it, but there was no question she felt it too. The pull between them, thick as taffy on a summer day. A slow, sexy song began to play, and the guests all clapped and stomped, calling their names.

"Get on with it, Romeo." She had her serious RN voice on now and for some twisted reason, the disparity between that and her body language raised his blood pressure higher, making his cock pulse. Sharp-witted and strong-willed, which he respected in so many ways. But in the bedroom, she'd be all his.

He bit back a curse, shut down his brain altogether, and focused every ounce of his energy on the task at hand. No time for thinking. It was time to get a garter on a bridesmaid. Not the Courtney he knew who'd wormed her vanilla way into his rocky road dreams. Just some girl on a chair.

Sitting right in front of him.

Lips parted.

Pulse pounding.
Pink-cheeked.
Shit.

He squeezed his eyes closed and took her leg in hand to circle her slim ankle. Lightly at first, then, without conscious thought, more firmly, letting her feel his strength. She gasped, and his eyes snapped open.

He tried, god knew he tried to fight it, but it was like his hands had a mind of their own, desperate to make her gasp again, desperate to take her further as he slid to the side, taking her ankle with him. A scant few inches that would be imperceptible to onlookers, but that Courtney no doubt felt, as the move spread her legs for him. Not wide. Just open enough to make her aware of her position. Just open enough to let her know what was on his mind…what he really wanted from her in that moment.

Watch yourself, his mind blared.

But he was too far gone.

He kept his gaze trained on her face as he tightened his fingers into a band of resistance, effectively restraining her, and slid the garter over her foot and onto her calf. Her throat worked visibly, her body tensing as she opened her mouth to say something, but she closed it with a snap. He lifted her leg high then, resting her ankle on his shoulder and pinning it there with his hand.

The crowd squealed with excitement and laughter, caught up in the bawdy tradition and outward bravado of the moment, but the look on Courtney's face was anything but funny. Her lush bottom lip was caught between her teeth and her eyes lit with fire so hot it nearly brought him low.

And what was so much worse?

She didn't pull away.

Chapter Two

Panic warred with bone-deep need as Courtney stared down into the face that had dominated her thoughts for weeks now. His jaw was set tight, his gaze so intense, she couldn't help but wonder what it would feel like to be the true focus of that intensity. Naked. On a bed. Heck, on a floor, for that matter.

A peal of laughter—Lacey's?—broke through the sensual spell Rafe had woven over her, and she shook her head briskly.

This wasn't right. None of it. Her enjoyment of his sure grip. Her twisted desire to offer up her other foot for the more of the same. The wild thoughts of him switching places with her, planting his fine ass on this frou-frou chair and dragging her over his lap.

For what? her subconscious whispered. So that he could *spank* her?

Her body tensed, and a bolt of lightning zinged through her before settling right between her thighs. Panic escalated as she jerked against his unyielding fingers.

"People are watching, Court," he murmured. "You getting up and tearing ass out of here will look really strange.

I know you're nervous and afraid of what you're feeling, but trust me, I'd never do anything you didn't want me to."

His eyes shone with absolute sincerity, and she willed herself to settle back in.

He was right. It was one thing to escape for a minute before the festivities had begun. It was something else entirely to run away from what would appear to onlookers as nothing more than a campy wedding tradition.

They had no way of knowing that she was falling to pieces on the inside.

"Fine. Then what I want is for you to get on with it, for Pete's sake."

He tipped his head to the side and nodded slowly before sliding the garter up her leg without further ado. It settled into place over her thigh, and she steeled herself for his touch on the way down, but he was careful to avoid even incidental contact.

"Your wish is my command." A second later, he set her foot gently back onto the ground, sat back on his haunches, and settled the skirt of her dress back into place.

The music faded out and she forced a smile as the crowd clapped enthusiastically. He'd done exactly as she'd asked and, finally, it was over.

So why did she feel so bereft?

Before she could think too hard on the answer to that question, a loud voice rang in her ear.

"Whew! You guys were like something out of an Animal Planet documentary for a minute out there," Cat said, yanking her up from the chair. Rafe stood, offering a mocking half grin and sweeping bow in their direction before gesturing toward the bar.

"Now that the garter is safely hidden away, can I get you ladies a drink?"

Courtney pressed a hand to her heated cheeks and

mumbled a "no thanks," adding a head shake in case he couldn't hear her.

Maybe it was a combination of looks and confidence, or maybe it was the almost palpable sexuality of the man topped off with the aura of raw, masculine power, but whatever it was, she literally couldn't handle it, and he knew it. She needed to regroup.

"I just got a fresh one," Cat said, holding up a glassful of ruby-red liquid. "But thanks."

Courtney allowed her friend to lead her away to a quiet corner where she pinned her with her an all-too-perceptive gaze.

"You know, Rafe is part of the crew. You're going to have to figure out whatever this is between you and either get past it or grab on to it. Better now than letting it drag out." She flicked a look over her shoulder in Rafe's direction and waggled her eyebrows comically. "And if you were smart, you'd be all about the grabbing on to it. He's almost as cute as Shane."

Courtney managed a halfhearted snort of faux-disgust. "Are you for real right now? You know what he's into. This is the kind of stuff that sets feminism back a hundred years." She set her bouquet on the linen-covered table and tried not to cringe at the shrill piousness in her voice, wondering who exactly she was trying to convince.

After weeks of trying to stay atop her high horse, she'd finally accepted that her issues weren't with Rafe's lifestyle at all. The bluster was just a bunch of meaningless words now, thrown up like shields to deflect from the real crux of the matter. Spankings and handcuffs didn't scare her. Relationships scared her. Getting lost in a man again—especially one so strong, one who would be so easy to get lost in—that was what had her shaking in her shoes. But she wasn't about to admit that to Cat.

Her friend shook her head violently, sending her brassy curls swinging. "You are so wrong. Sure, I wouldn't put up with a guy bossing me out of bed, but in the bedroom?" She shrugged and grinned. "It's kinda hot. When Shane goes a little alpha on me, I get all melty. Seriously, you shouldn't knock it until you try it."

She crossed her arms over her chest to chase away the odd chill that had sneaked up on her. "I'm pretty sure we're not talking about your run-of-the-mill, occasional-furry-handcuff stuff here, Cat. I think it's more than that."

Lie. She *knew* it was more than that. Even during their three-minute interaction on the dance floor, she could feel the strength of his will winding its way around her, tugging her toward some dark, hidden place. What if it grew deeper, into something more than sexual control?

Emotional currency. That's what she couldn't afford to gamble with again.

It had happened so slowly with Wes. Over the course of eighteen months. First, it was "making sure everyone had everyone else's e-mail and computer passwords." A "good-faith gesture to foster a feeling of trust and mutual respect." Then it was making sure everyone was being considerate by calling to confirm that it was okay to make plans that didn't involve the other person. And so it went.

Not once in the first year did any of it raise a single red flag. She blindly followed along, thinking how much more efficient and civilized their relationship was compared to other couples around them. Until the two-way street became a one-way street and she found herself asking for permission to go the grocery store.

By the time she had reached point break and got the balls up to walk away, it was too late. When she was feeling heartsick and alone, she'd picked up the phone and realized there was no one left to call. Her friends had dropped off one by one after broken plans when Wes decided that she didn't need to go out after all, or unreturned calls when Wes had decided that she really had no use for her own cell phone anyway.

Courtney swallowed a sigh, wishing she could share her fears with Cat, but she wasn't ready to talk about Wes yet. Not because she didn't trust her friend, but because she was ashamed of her weakness…ashamed for letting it get as bad as it did.

"All joking aside, whatever you decide to do, make sure you're careful with Rafe," Cat said, concern chasing the smile from her usually laughing eyes. "I'm all about having fun, but as much as I love him, he's not the kind of guy that sticks. Not anymore, at least."

Had Rafe gotten hurt before too? Courtney's heart tripped at the sadness on Cat's face. Before she could press her for the details she wasn't sure she really wanted to know, their tipsy bride burrowed between them, face aglow.

"Come and do the Electric Slide with me! Hurry, before it's over," Lacey said.

Courtney pushed aside the melancholy thoughts and took Lacey's hand, and the three of them headed back to the dance floor. They'd dance a while, get through the cake ritual, and before she knew it, people would be saying their good-byes, with her leading the pack. Galen and Lacey had a flight to catch in a couple of hours, in any case, so there was a definite expiration time to her misery and confusion.

Then, with Cat's blessing or without it, Operation Avoidance was in full effect, at least until she fortified her defenses after this recent breech.

Yup, as long as she stayed out of the path of Hurricane Davenport for a few weeks, everything would be A-okay.

Nooo sweat.

• • •

Rafe blew out a long sigh and tightened his grip on the steering wheel, trying not to remember how it felt when he'd tightened that same grip over Courtney's silky ankle. It was going to be another long night fueled by erotic dreams. After touching all that smooth skin, it was a given. He was going to have to put some serious time and effort into solving this problem, because it was really starting to impact his life.

With a growl of frustration, he clicked on the radio. Maybe some loud music would drown out his thoughts. He'd gone a whole three minutes without thinking about her when a dim light ahead caught his attention. He frowned through his windshield as he sidled up to a familiar silver coupe off to the side of the dark, tree-lined road.

What were the fucking odds?

He bit back a groan and pulled over, slowing to a stop before popping it into park.

Courtney had left the reception a good thirty minutes before him, and now here she was, sitting in her car, illuminated only by the light of her cell phone, on which she was tapping away. What was so damned important that it couldn't wait until she got home? A booty call, maybe?

The thought shouldn't have sent a bolt of annoyance through him, but it did. Her sex life wasn't any of his concern, and she was entitled to all the booty she could wrangle up. No skin off his ass. Maybe her pulling over on a narrow, deserted road a wink away from full-on nighttime with no streetlights around wasn't the brightest of ideas, but he guessed it beat the hell out of texting and driving.

Still, he wasn't about to let her stay there if he could help it. He fumbled in his glove box for a second and then stuck the police lights onto the roof, flicking them on before pulling around in front of her.

He left the lights flashing as he got out and strode to her car. The window slid down, and she glared at him.

"Is that really necessary?" she muttered, setting the phone aside.

"Necessary?" He considered that, and her pretty, flushed face, for a long moment before shaking his head slowly. "Maybe not, but if someone comes around that corner less than alert, they could clip your back end. At least this way they'll see the lights flashing."

She chewed her bottom lip and looked away. "Fine. When you leave, I'll put my hazards on."

He leaned in and unlocked her car door from the inside, smothering a chuckle as she leaned back as far as the stick shift would allow her to. "I'm not going to molest you, Courtney." Opening the door, he gestured for her to step out. "Unless of course, you want me to."

She gave him the dead eyes and swung her legs onto the pavement.

"Can you turn the lights off, please?" She poked a finger toward the dash and popped on her hazards. "If someone I know drives by they're going to think I'm getting arrested."

Since two of the four people from the wedding who would've been taking that particular road back home were en route to the airport, and the other two had opted to spend the night in the cabin, there was a pretty good chance no one they knew was going to happen by, but that wasn't his concern at the moment.

"Should you be driving?" He vaguely recalled her drinking a couple glasses of wine early on, and a glass of champagne that Cat had given her, but once cake had been served, she'd seemed much more interested in staring steadfastly into her coffee mug for the last hour or so than interacting with anyone or merrymaking.

"I'm fine. If I wasn't, I would've stayed overnight at the cabin with Cat and Shane."

He eyed her assessingly, and she pursed her lips.

"Did you need to give me a sobriety test, Officer?"

"It's Detective, remember?" He helped her out of the car, part of him annoyed by her wisecracks, the other part thinking of all the ways he could put that mouth to better use if only she saw things his way.

"Okay, *Detective*. But for your information, I was driving fine until a rabbit ran in front of me and I swerved into the curb to avoid it and punctured my tire. I was waiting for a call back from roadside assistance when you stopped to harass me."

Lucky she hadn't swerved and hit a tree. She should've taken her chances with the rabbit and dealt with the guilt. Better a dead bunny than having to be wrenched out of a scrap of twisted metal via Jaws of Life and carted to a hospital. He opened his mouth to tell her that, but then snapped it shut.

She clearly wasn't in the mood for a lecture, and he was already on the edge of doing something stupid. No need to guarantee it by getting into some sort of pissing contest with her that could only end in more fireworks between them.

He wound his way around to the passenger's side of the car, and she followed behind.

Eyeing the obliterated tire, he nodded. "Yep, that's flat, all right. But you can call the place back and cancel. I'll change it for you as long as you have a spare."

"That's *one* option," she agreed. "Or I could continue to sit here doing just fine all by myself and wait a few minutes for them to get back to me while I dominate at Words With Friends." She looked very pleased with herself until her choice of words registered and then she started to stutter. "Like…not *dominate* dominate. But I'm good at it. Words With Friends, I mean. On my cell phone."

"I knew what you meant." He'd almost convinced himself to let her off the hook, but the devil took hold of him again.

"I'm good at it, too. And I *don't* mean Words With Friends."

She blinked up at him, the pink tip of her tongue flicking out to wet her lips, catching his attention, making him wish she would use it on him.

Anywhere.

Everywhere.

She cleared her throat, crossing her arms over her chest, and the move sent her breasts plumping up to strain the sweetheart neckline of her dress. "Why are you doing this?" she asked, her husky voice making his cock swell against the fly of his tuxedo pants.

"Doing what?" He moved closer, like a fish on a hook, drawn to her in a way he couldn't explain, never mind control. He didn't stop until they were only a foot apart, and she craned her neck to look up at him.

"That," she said, her voice breaking. "This." She waved a fluttering hand back and forth between them. "Don't play dumb, Rafe. You know exactly what I mean. Why do you keep toying with me?"

The air crackled, and the sound of insects chirping filled the air, amplified by their deafening silence. *Walk away,* his brain supplied helpfully, almost frantically. *Just walk away.* But the rest of him didn't get the memo because his feet wouldn't cooperate.

Instead, his stupid mouth took the lead. "Hell if I know," he said, shaking his head slowly. His feet chose that moment to start working again and closed the last of the gap between them. The deepest part of him reveled in her gasp as their thighs bumped.

"I'd love to take the blame for"—he mimicked her hand motion—"*this*. And frankly, if it was all me, it would be easy to stop. But it's not, is it?"

"It is," she insisted, but her face told another story.

"No. You and I did fine together before." He was close

enough to catch the scent of her light perfume, and it made his head swim with the need to press his face to her nape and breathe her in more deeply. "The tension was there, but we kept our distance and still managed to hang with the group, no problem." Aside from him fantasizing about her, but he didn't view that as a problem, and that wasn't the point. *What was the point again?* "The point is, before a couple weeks ago, you didn't know what I was into, nor did you care. It wasn't something I talked about, and it wasn't like I tried to convert you to my way of thinking."

No sense mentioning that he'd considered doing exactly that on more than one occasion.

"Then you changed toward me the instant you heard—secondhand, I might add—that I like to dominate my women sexually."

The growing panic on her face fled and she lifted her chin. "See?" She poked him in the chest with her pointer finger. "You said 'my women.' That's so archaic. It's the twenty-first century. A woman doesn't *belong* to anyone." Her gaze was triumphant, her stance aggressive and chock-full of "gotcha there."

That would probably have been a deterrent to a lot of guys. Her refusal to accept what was right in front of her. Her need to pretend that she wasn't at least curious and at most enthralled with the notion of the two of them. There were plenty of women out there who didn't need any convincing.

But unfortunately, ever since she'd gotten in his head, he didn't want other women. He wanted this one, and she wanted him.

Maybe it was because his nature wouldn't allow him to leave a gauntlet unretrieved on the ground between them. Maybe it was because he knew he had the key to unlocking something that had clearly been trapped in her for so long. Hell, maybe it was because she was so fucking beautiful and the thought of her on her knees in front of him, begging for more of whatever he had to give, made his cock hard enough to cut glass. Whatever the case, he sure as hell couldn't bring himself to walk away.

Not yet.

His intent must have shown on his face because her self-satisfied smirk slid away, and her eyes went wide.

"Rafe, listen, I—"

"I think I've done enough listening," he murmured, pressing closer until he could feel her breath on his jaw. "Now it's your turn." He cupped her hips and flipped her around roughly, pressing her into the hood of the car, using his thighs as leverage. He bent low, curling his body over hers until his mouth was a scant inch from her ear.

"Make no mistake," he breathed, letting his lips brush the soft skin of her jaw, exulting in her full-body shudder. "I might not be in the market for love, but any woman who wants to sleep with me will absolutely and unequivocally be *my* woman in the bedroom. If she's not? If she can't trust me to give her everything she needs…everything she could possibly want? Then I've failed her."

The breath sawed in and out of her lungs, but she didn't struggle. In fact, she didn't move at all. She seemed to be waiting for something. His pulse accelerated as he kneaded her hips gently. Then he felt it. Pressure against his groin as she flexed her ass ever so slightly back against him. His balls drew tight and his cock thickened.

She might be too stubborn to say it, but her body told him everything he needed to know. She wanted more, and far be it from him to deny her.

He flexed forward, grinding his erection against her bottom as his hands traveled up her rib cage to skate over the sides of her full breasts. He didn't stop, lacing her fingers with his and dragging her hands up the hood of the car until they were high over her head.

She let out a catchy moan. "Rafe—"

It was scary, how bad he wanted her. Scary enough that he was starting to have second thoughts himself, but he couldn't bring himself to pull the plug. She had to be the one to stop this, or there would be no stopping.

A warm summer breeze kicked up as he clamped his fingers tight around her wrists and pinned her to the hood with his hips, hard enough to make her gasp.

"Say the word, Court. Tell me no, and we both walk away, no harm, no foul." He pressed his chest against her back until her torso and cheek were flush against the car and she let out a squeak. The blood rushed to his ears as a dozen scenarios ran through his head, each more erotic than the last.

"Tell me no," he murmured against the soft shell of her ear, "and I won't slide my hands up that little dress and work that pussy until you scream."

Her legs began to tremble against his, but still she stayed silent. A roar of masculine satisfaction built in his chest, but he beat it back, intent on making sure he offered one final out before he allowed the shit to truly hit the fan.

"Last warning, cupcake." He trailed his hand down her bare arm, snaking it between the hood and her breast, before teasing the pebbled nipple that jutted against his fingers. "Tell me no, or I'm going to make you come. And then when it's over? I'll do it again."

Chapter Three

The silence remained, but this time it was filled with a promise, as clear and true as a song.

She wasn't going to stop him.

Elation rolled through him like a drug, clouding his senses. He tugged the peak of her breast again then, hard enough that she felt it. She tensed and moaned, making it impossible to hear anything over the blood pounding in his ears. She might not know it yet, but she was ripe for this. For someone—no, not someone, he thought fiercely, for *him*—to teach her what her body already knew.

She craved it. The pleasure and the pain. The ability to give herself over completely.

Now if only he could impart her first lesson without coming in his pants, they'd be golden. He refused to think about tomorrow.

He wedged his knee between her thighs, spreading them wide enough that he could press his cock in the cleft between her ass cheeks. He thrust hard against her, letting her feel his need, before pulling back. With a deliberateness that had him shaking with the effort, he straightened and traced his hands down her sides until he reached her full hips again.

He loved that about her. She was fit for sure, but her curves were luscious; he couldn't wait to get his hands on them. He stepped back and, with a flick of his wrists, he flipped up her skirt, baring her smooth, round ass cheeks to his hungry gaze, interrupted only by the peach lace thong nestled between them.

The red and blue flashing lights from his police siren dappled her ivory skin, and the urge to replace those marks with some of his own gripped him like a boa constrictor. If he was home, he'd use a mini-deerskin…start slow. Easy. Let her get used to the sting. Then he'd work his way up.

He traced the scrap of panties with his fingertips, lower and lower still until he reached her core. Fuck, she was soaked. He growled low in his throat and she let out a hiss as he stroked her, hard and deep, through the wet satin.

"That's good, Court. Really good. Scoot up now, until your feet are off the ground." It wasn't a suggestion. In spite of his praise, his tone was all demand, and again, he waited with bated breath for her reaction, well aware that at any time, something could trigger her to call it quits.

She didn't hesitate, shimmying forward, skin squeaking against the hood as she did his bidding. He dragged his gaze from her glorious ass because if he didn't, he wasn't sure he could stop himself from freeing his cock from his pants and plunging into her until they both saw stars.

Instead, he took a long, slow breath and stared down at her. Ass up, lips parted, eyes squeezed closed as her fingers scrabbled at the gleaming silver of the hood while he stroked her hot slit.

"Please," she whispered, her hips pulsing now, urging him to dip his fingers deeper. The motion brought the garter he'd placed high on her thigh into view and his stomach tightened.

"I need—"

He sent one long digit past the soaked scrap between her thighs and thrust it into her. She bucked back against him, but it was the way that her walls gripped him so perfectly that made his balls ache with pressure to finish the deed. It was exactly that grinding need that made him pull back and return to low, teasing thrusts.

She protested, wriggling and making soft, pleading sounds in the back of her throat, but he didn't give in. He couldn't be trusted with her orgasms if he couldn't manage his own.

"Rafe, I can't wait." She sounded close to tears and it jarred him from his thoughts. "Please, just…"

He didn't waste time contemplating the hows or whys of it. Courtney had reached her tipping point. He was a hard man, but he wasn't a monster.

He closed his fist around the offending scrap between them and yanked. Her panties came away with a snap, and he shoved them in his pocket before sliding his fingers back between her legs, coating them in her silky wetness. Calling on every ounce of restraint, he focused on her body's response to his touch, adjusting the pressure, massaging her clit until she couldn't keep from moving with him.

"I want you to come now, Court. Make it hard. Make it loud. Make it pretty for me." He tucked one finger inside her, hard and deep, curling it until it butted against her G-spot with every thrust.

"Oh my God, Rafe, please, f—" She jammed her knuckles into her mouth and muttered incoherently as he worked his finger in and out, harder and faster. Her body quaked and shook.

"Move your hand. I want to hear you." His words were clear but mustn't have registered, so he repeated them with an accompanying firm slap on the ass to get her attention.

The crack resounded through the trees and echoed back. She froze, but not before shudders racked her from head to toe. He waited for a long moment, and his patience was rewarded as she flexed her ass up higher in the universal sign for "Please sir, can I have some more."

Even the forest seemed to hold its breath as he raised his hand high, and sent it screaming down to connect with the smooth flesh of her ass a second time. Her juices soaked his hand and he thrust a second finger to join the first, plunging them deep and deeper still as a low, keening sound built in her throat. Then she exploded, her tight pussy clenching and releasing over his fingers as she screamed. His cock leaped, heaving against its confines with the need to join her, but he managed to regain his focus, working her through her climax, keeping his strokes long and steady until she finally stopped bucking.

The sounds of their combined harsh breathing reached his ears as she quieted and he slid his hand from her still-molten core. He hadn't worked out any plan past this moment, and his brain had ceased to function due to lack of blood flow anywhere but south.

He patted her gently on the ass and stepped back, every nerve in his body straining against the need to finish it. To pound into her until he came so hard, he couldn't see straight.

She stirred, slowly at first, then with clear intent, scrabbling backward toward him until her feet touched the ground. Eyes still glassy as she drifted downward, nearly to her knees.

It went against every instinct to stop her when he wanted nothing more than to let her take him in her mouth right now. But if they went further, it would be because she'd had the time and the mental awareness to think it through, not because she was still addled by their unquestionably mind-boggling chemistry. "No."

She blinked up at him, seeming to come back into herself, and her cheeks reddened. "I want…"

He tugged her to her feet, wondering how much to say. He needn't have worried because a shrill sound came from inside the car, saving him the immediate trouble.

"That's…" She cleared her throat and tried again, righting her dress with a fluttering hand. "That's my phone."

She shouldered past him without meeting his gaze and yanked open the passenger's-side door.

A second later, she answered the call with a shrill, "Hello?"

He adjusted himself in his pants, even the utilitarian touch adding to his ache, as she replied to the person on the other end of the line.

"Thank you so much, I'll keep an eye out." Her gratitude was so effusive, her body language so stiff and standoffish, he didn't need her to tell him that her automotive guardian angel was on the way, and that she could hardly wait to be rescued from the big bad wolf now that she'd regained her senses. A pang of disappointment hit him harder than he was comfortable with.

She disconnected and squared her shoulders before facing him.

"Well, that was good timing, I guess." It took him a second to get the words out past the thickness in his throat, and when he did, they were less casual-sounding than he'd hoped. In fact, he sounded like he'd swallowed a cactus.

Luckily—or not, depending on how he chose to look at it—she was too caught up in her own regret and desire to get rid of him to notice. "A minute sooner, and that would have been a damned shame."

Although, he was still pretty pissed off that he'd been forced to break a promise. He'd told her he'd make her come and then come again. She wasn't his woman, but if she was, that phone would've gone unanswered until he'd made good on his vow.

She looked away, giving him her profile in the moonlight. Her lips were swollen, probably from biting them, or maybe from her knuckles mashing the tender flesh against her teeth. Either way, he couldn't take the credit no matter how much he wanted to. They'd never even kissed, a fact that annoyed him now as he stared at her.

Tousled honey curls and heaving breasts derailed his thoughts. The grinding need to press her to her knees into the soft grass and fuck that sweet mouth until he exploded against the back of her throat and she sucked him dry. His cock pulsed, and he felt a thick, salty tear escape the swollen head as he ran his still-damp index finger over her bottom lip.

"That"—he gestured to the hood of the car—"was beautiful. I don't know why you've chosen to be without a man for so long, and I'm not going to ask you to tell me. But know this. We could be great together."

He took a step forward and she took a step back, holding him off with a hand on his chest that would have been much more convincing if she hadn't caressed his pectoral muscle for an instant before stilling.

"I'm not in a good place right now," she admitted softly. "I don't even know who I am anymore. I feel so lost. I can't be in a relationship until I figure out how I went so wrong in the last one."

He knew what it was to be lost. He'd felt that way since the day Monica died. The only difference between him and Courtney was that she wanted to be found again someday. Not him. He'd been in love before and knew one thing for sure. That would be the first and last time. Nothing was worth going through that kind of pain again.

He pushed away the bitter sadness that always came with thoughts of his past and focused on the now. "I don't do relationships either, but that doesn't mean I'm going to live like a priest."

She shook her head slowly. "Don't you feel bad doing that to the women you're with?"

"Bad about what? A mutually pleasurable exchange? The rules are set out front so everybody's eyes are open. I keep it to four scenes, max, with the understanding before we ever start that it will never be more. We're all adults. I don't see the victim here."

Curiosity seemed to pull her from the melancholy and she blinked up at him. "Why four scenes?"

"Any more than that, things tend to get…sticky, no matter how clearly expectations are laid out." It had taken him a few tries and one set of slashed tires to get the formula exactly right, but since then, his partners had been content, and so had he.

But right now, he was the furthest thing from content. For some reason he couldn't explain, he needed to know that he'd be able to touch this woman again more than he needed air.

"I believe we can help each other, Courtney. You can help me get you out of my head, and I can help give you back your confidence, teach you to trust again, in the purest sense. That's the beauty of a power exchange. It's all about trust on both sides."

He could see her wavering, taking his words in and letting them settle.

"A contract. Four scenes. Sex only."

"It all seems so clinical," she murmured, but she didn't say no.

"Believe me, it will be anything but that. You want to trust yourself again? Start now. Go with your gut. I dare you." He'd wondered if she'd been friends with Cat and Lacey long enough for the gravity of those three words to hit home, but her gasp answered his question. His crew took dares very seriously and so, apparently, did she. "Four scenes," he pressed. "Me and you."

She opened her mouth, but he held up a hand.

"Don't decide now. Think about it. The next time I see you, I'll expect an answer. Know this, though. If you pass, I won't ask again."

The sound of an engine echoed, and lights flashed in the distance. The tow truck had made good time. Too good. He could sense her pulling away from him already.

Her now-focused hazel eyes were as pleading as her tone, and she backed away from him.

"You need to go now." Her voice was muffled as she turned. "This was a mistake. That girl? That's not me."

He walked back to his car, her final words settling over him like dank smog. If they were true, it would've been a damned shame. Because that girl?

He'd walk through hell to have her in his bed.

Chapter Four

"So wait, first and most importantly, is it huge?"

Courtney couldn't stop her crack of laughter as she met Cat's lively green gaze in the bathroom mirror. The release of tension felt good. She'd been a walking ball of nerves for the past ten days, terrified of running into Rafe somewhere with no idea what she'd say to him when she did. Add to that a shit day at the hospital with her new boss, and a girl's night out with Cat was exactly what she needed.

They'd been at Sully's for less than an hour when a couple beers had loosened her tongue, and Cat had all but dragged her into the restroom to get the dirty details on Rafe.

"Well, spill it, woman!"

The apples of her cheeks grew pink and she shrugged. "I didn't see *it*. I didn't see much of anything. I was…" She lowered her voice to whisper and peered around before continuing, "…facedown on the car most of the time the good stuff was happening."

Cat's delighted guffaw echoed through the room, and Courtney shushed her furiously.

"We're the only ones here, doofus. So what's this about facedown?" Cat swept a paper towel over the sink area to dry off a spot and hoisted her trim frame up to perch there, legs folded crisscross. "There is literally no possibility of you leaving this bathroom until you elaborate." Her eyes narrowed as Courtney's gaze flickered to the door. "You feeling froggy, then jump, but I'll tell you right now, you'll never make it. You're in espadrilles, I'm in flat sandals. I'll take you down like a fucking gazelle if I have to."

Courtney didn't doubt it, but she was still weighing her options, unsure whether reliving the encounter out loud would be more or less painful than the gazelle thing, when a knock sounded at the door.

"Someone in there?" a high-pitched voice called.

The relief must have been evident on her face because Cat slashed her hand across her own throat in warning before calling back, "Yes. And sorry, it's going to be a while. Bad Thai food." She added a long, loud groan for good measure. "There's another single-stall bathroom behind the dance floor."

Her declaration was met with silence and then the retreating *clickety-click* of heels on hardwood. After a few seconds, she beckoned Courtney with a hand before propping her chin on her fists like a child waiting for a bedtime story. "Continue."

Courtney sank into the tiny vanity chair in the corner with a resigned sigh. There had been a time, before she'd moved to New England last year and met Shane and his friends, that a conversation like this would have been impossible. A time where she didn't have one friend left to go out for drinks or gossip about guys with. Because of Wes.

Her stomach churned as she remembered those days, and she shoved the dark thoughts aside. She was here now, and she had four great friends and one...whatever the hell Rafe was. The point was, she *wanted* to share the good stuff with Cat. Maybe talking it through would give her some previously unattainable clarity.

"Okay, so what did I already tell you?"

"Nothing," Cat said with a snort of disgust. "You said you had an 'uncomfortable conversation,' and then things got weird and you stopped coming around like a butt-face."

She deserved that jab. She'd skipped last Friday's happy hour and a day trip to the lake in an effort to avoid Rafe, and Cat was rightfully irritated by the blow-offs. Hopefully, once she laid it all out for her, she'd understand. Act one of learning to trust again was starting now. She took a slug of her beer and settled more deeply into her dainty seat. This was going to take a while.

"It really started at the reception," she began slowly, trying not to give any credence to the bubbly sensation rising in her chest as she told the story. So strange that she'd expected being dominated would remind her of what it was like to feel weak, because in those moments with Rafe, she'd never felt sexier or stronger.

By the time she got to the part where he tore off her underwear, she was grinning like a teenage girl with her first major crush, and Cat was gaping at her, wide-eyed.

"So. Hot," she whispered, her fingers fluttering at her throat.

"You don't know the half of it. The things he said." Courtney fanned her heated face and shook her head, at a loss as to how to put her feelings into words. "The way he said them…"

"He made you feel like you were the sexiest, most desirable woman on earth," Cat whispered reverently, a secret smile tugging at her lips. "Shane does that too, although maybe not quite the same way. But it's awesome."

Cat's drawing correlations between her relationship with

her husband-to-be and Courtney's own one-night not-quite fling with Rafe served as a much-needed slap back to reality.

"Not the same thing," she said, clearing her throat and springing to her feet. "Anyway," she chirped brightly. "You wanted to know why I've been scarce. That's the reason. We parted ways, but not before he issued a challenge of sorts. Next time I see him, I'm supposed to tell him whether I want to do a few scenes with him, or forget it ever happened." *As if.*

Cat nodded, but looked a little green around the gills. "Wow. That's big."

"Are you okay? You look nauseous."

"Nope, I'm good. So, um, have you thought about what you're going to do? You know, if you, like, run into him?"

The better question was, had she thought of anything else? She shrugged and led the way out the door, back into the bar, and Cat followed. "Of course. But I'm trying to keep a clear head. It's sucked not being able to come around, and if we hook up, I'm nervous things will get weird between us after it's over, and it will screw up the group dynamic more than it already has." *And because I'm scared shitless of how he makes me feel*, she stopped herself from adding. Trust was one thing; baring her soul, even to her friend, would have to wait for another day.

"There's always been tension between you. Probably won't be any weirder than before," Cat hedged, slowing her pace until Courtney had to stop altogether to avoid yelling down the hall to respond.

"Well, luckily, I can take as much time as I need to think about it. When Lacey gets back from her honeymoon, the three of us can hang out and stuff, but I'll avoid the boys until I'm sure."

She kept her tone light, but she felt a bit deflated...hollow inside. Saying it all out loud and sharing what had happened between her and Rafe had felt good at the time, but now it only served as yet another reminder of how amazing it had been.

And she hadn't even told her friend the best/worst part.

After too many solo close calls to calculate, and encounters with boyfriends that had started off so promising but fizzled out too soon, her sexual journey in life had been an exercise in frustration. Until that night when, in less than fifteen minutes, with seemingly no effort at all, Rafe Davenport had used his magic hands to gift her with her first and only orgasm.

Ever.

She was factoring that little reminder in with the rest of her jumbled list of pros and cons when Cat grabbed her arm and squeezed, pulling her to a stop.

"Listen, Court, there's something I have to tell you." Her friend's face was pinched with worry and Courtney's stomach did a free fall. "And I'm pretty sure you're gonna be mad."

• • •

"You want to split a pitcher or you want a scotch?" Shane called over his shoulder as he made his way to the bar.

"Surprise me." Rafe picked up his third and final dart, briefly considering whether to walk up to the board and bury it dead-center when Shane wasn't looking just to fuck with him. He opted against it, mainly because he was feeling pretty grateful to the guy. His phone call had saved him another night prowling around the house, restless as a caged lion.

Work was stressful, but that was standard during the hotter months. As the temperature rose, so did people's tempers, and violent crimes skyrocketed. But if he was being honest with himself, it was more than that. Ever since he'd laid the dare at Courtney's pretty feet he could think of little else. He imagined—or hoped, maybe?—that she was in the same bad way, although it didn't seem likely. If her absence was any indicator, she'd either settled on a nonverbal "no" or was avoiding him like the plague.

Neither option sat well with him, and his relief at getting out of the house evaporated instantly. Maybe it was time to admit defeat and move on. He cocked his wrist and let the dart fly just as a low gasp sounded behind him.

His pulse sped as he turned to see Courtney standing by the hallway leading to the restroom. If her flushed cheeks and shocked eyes were any indication, she hadn't expected him to be there.

Cat stepped between them and waved. "Hey, Rafe! You're here. I wasn't sure you guys were coming." She scrubbed her pert nose—maybe to stop it from growing?—and offered him a shaky grin.

Before Rafe could respond, Shane strode toward them, pitcher of lager in hand.

"Hey, babe." He checked out his fiancée, oblivious to the melodrama playing out around him, and let out a low whistle. "You look gorgeous tonight." He slung his free arm around her and pulled her close for a quick, hard kiss.

Cat scrambled away and shot a miserable look in Courtney's direction as she took the pitcher from her man and set it on the long oak table. "Why don't we go see Sully and get me and Courtney a couple frosted glasses?"

He waved her off with a grin. "Sit, I'll get…" He trailed off at her pointed glare and sent her a puzzled look before nodding. "Yeah, sure. Not clear on why this is a two-man job, but let's do it."

She rolled her eyes, mumbling something as she tugged him toward the bar. A second later, Rafe was alone with Courtney.

He dug deep for a tight smile, but it was rough going because she looked distractingly spectacular. Heels, naturally, just to twist the knife a little. Wedge sandals, to be exact, in a rainbow of colors that made him think of sunshine. And fucking. He worked his way from the bottom up, taking in her tight little body, dressed for the ninety-degree heat in shorts that made him hope a game of pool was in their future and a lemon-yellow halter top that clung to her curves in the best way. Her long thick hair was high up in a sloppy topknot that had him instantly fantasizing about taking it down.

Or commanding her to take it down for him once he stripped her bare so he could watch those locks tumble loose in a silky waterfall over her full, ripe—

He put that thought on lock, quick. No point in waiting. He was nothing if not a man of his word, and he'd already broken one vow he'd made to her. He'd keep this one whether she wanted him to or not.

"So what's it going to be?"

She clearly had no clue he was going to be there, and he waited for the platitudes he knew were coming. Maybe she'd give some bland excuse about a hazardous coffeepot she'd neglected to turn off. Or maybe she'd stay for a few minutes to be polite and then fake an emergency at the hospital.

But he couldn't have been more wrong.

Instead, she stared at him like he was a scorpion guarding a cheesecake. A mixture of longing and fear played over her rounded features, and he resisted the urge to comfort her. Offer her more time. But sometimes the best decisions were the ones made when a person relied on their gut to provide the answer instead of letting their thoughts complicate matters.

Time for your gut check, Courtney.

"I'm not trying to be difficult," he said softly. "I can leave if you're not comfortable." Because he was a gentleman and she'd obviously been brought here under false pretenses. "Once you've given me your answer, of course." Okay, so maybe not that much of a gentleman. "Yes or no, cupcake."

"Why do you keep calling me cupcake?" She wet her lip and shifted from foot to foot.

Stall tactics. He considered her question and shrugged. There was no harm in answering. "Well, first off, cupcakes can be vanilla, like you. But they're also sweet—" He stepped closer and let his gaze trail over her from head to heel. "Pretty to look at, and I can't be within ten feet of one without wanting to taste it."

She looked around the room as if searching for an escape route, but when she met his gaze again, she seemed calmer. More at ease. This was it. She was going to say no and walk away. The tiny part of him that felt like he was fooling himself, that all the planning in the world wouldn't stop this woman from somehow wreaking havoc on his life, felt relieved, while the rest of him ached.

But she threw him for a loop yet again. "You said it had to be the next time I saw you." Her tone was matter-of-fact, and the wariness was gone from her eyes. "I'm still seeing you. You're right in front of me. I should get until the end of the night." She tipped her chin in challenge and waited.

He admired her spunk so much he almost let her get away with it. Instead, he pressed, running on instinct.

"Four separate occasions, at my discretion, chosen from a previously agreed-upon list of possibilities, with the understanding that full-on intercourse is at your discretion. I can't promise it will change your mind," he said softly, leaning in close to make sure only she could hear, "but I promise to make you come so hard, you can't see straight. Over and over. And you can take that to the bank. Last chance, Courtney. Going once." Her lashes fluttered rapidly and she bit her lip. "Going twice..."

"Okay," she shouted before glancing around the room and lowering her voice. "Okay. I'm in."

Elation rushed through him, and he fought the basest of

instincts, compelling him to scoop her up and carry her out of the place. They still had a lot to work out, and he needed time to plan. He hadn't been overselling it when he'd told her that he wanted to help her, too. Teaching her to embrace the inner submissive she'd already given him a glimpse of was going to empower her in a way she couldn't fathom right now.

He had to make it perfect.

And when that niggling little part of him reared its head again, he smashed it down one last time. The details would be worked out beforehand, and there would be no i's undotted, no t's uncrossed.

It would be foolproof.

Chapter Five

The next day after work, Courtney found herself staring at Cat, still in semi-shock as her friend shoveled a forkful of Cobb salad into her mouth. She swiped a napkin over her lips and tapped the pen against her knuckle as she glanced down at her smartphone.

"Okay, we decided that double penetration is a hard no, right?"

Courtney didn't answer, the gravity of her circumstances becoming more apparent by the second. *What the hell had she been thinking?* With the dare in Rafe's eyes and the fear of letting an opportunity slip through her hands, combined with her own false bravado courtesy of Sam Adams, it had felt so right.

Terrifying, but right.

But in the light of day, sitting across from her friend with a sheaf of paper between them now riddled with salad dressing and words like "spanking" and "anal," she wondered if she'd lost her fucking mind.

"Courtney?"

"What?" she snapped back.

"You're still mad at me, aren't you?" Cat asked, leaning forward in her seat, the regret plain on her face. "If I'd known he'd given you an ultimatum or why you were avoiding him, I would never have told Shane and him it was okay to meet us. And once you told me…"

"It was too late. I know. I should've told you sooner, and I already said I wasn't mad. I'm just having buyer's remorse, is all."

"Come on, it's going to be fine. This is a generic list, something to give him a guideline. He probably isn't even into most of this stuff," Cat reassured her.

"Says you," she muttered miserably.

"This is exciting, remember? That's why you called me. You couldn't wait until tonight to start filling it out. Now buck up and let's have fun with it."

She hadn't been able to wait because of crippling anxiety seeping in once she'd received Rafe's e-mail that morning. Once she'd seen the kind of stuff on the survey he sent her, she'd needed Cat for moral support. But fun? No.

Fun was finding a twenty-dollar bill in a pair of jeans you hadn't worn in months. Fun was strawberry picking on a warm summer day and sneaking a few as you went. Sitting at a diner looking at a BDSM checklist online, sussing out the things she would or would not be okay doing with her new sex-on-the-edge instructor, and assigning them each a rating utilizing the world's most complex system that ranged from 1-5 but also included question marks, backslashes, and a capital X? That was the opposite of fun.

Cat sighed and set down her pen. "Look, let's finish the task at hand, okay? Rafe wants this scanned and e-mailed back to him tomorrow afternoon. If you decide you want to change something, you can do it in the morning after you sleep on it. And if you decide you want to back out altogether? You can still do that too. Just don't send him the list. No biggie, but at least let's get it all together so that if you do decide to go through with it, you're prepared, okay?" Her green eyes dimmed and she set her fork down. "Are you scared? If you're scared and want to change your mind already, fuck it, we don't need to—"

"Nope." Courtney shook her head and ran a finger around the rim of her water glass. "I'm not scared. Not of Rafe, at least. I'm scared of letting myself trust someone, though. It's been a long time since I've done that. And I've *never* done anything like this." Maybe it was time to come clean with the rest of it… "Rafe was my first."

Cat sat back against her chair so hard it tipped, almost flipping her onto her back. "Shut the front door!"

She shook her head furiously, "Wait, no, not my *first* first." She took a long pull from her glass and set it down before meeting her friend's curious gaze. "Before the other night, I'd never been able to…finish." The last was a whisper that seemed to hang in the air like a thundercloud.

"With a guy?" Cat asked, her brow wrinkled in confusion.

"At all," Courtney corrected sheepishly.

"Wowww…" She opened her mouth, seeming to gear up for a speech, but finally shook her head and repeated, "Wowww."

"Yeah, you said that."

"I know, but it deserved an echo. How did—" Cat held up both hands and started again. "Like, why didn't you—" She stopped again and shrugged helplessly. "Some guys suck, and some women are hard nuts to crack, so I guess that part's not that unusual, but did you not give it the old college try solo?"

"I gave it many, many tries. College tries. High school tries. Middle school tries. Summer camp tries." She toyed with the saltshaker absently. "It just seemed like the harder I chased it, the faster it ran."

Cat smiled then and patted her hand lightly. "And now Rafe…Jesus, I'm surprised you didn't knock him over the head and lock him in your basement."

That broke the tension as they busted out in giggles at the visual. "Believe me, I considered it."

"I bet. And this makes me more excited for you. You like him, right?"

Like was such a mild word for all the things she felt toward him. He pissed her off, and thrilled her and annoyed her and set her on fire all at the same time. But he was also a great guy. More than once, she'd seen him drop everything to help Shane or Galen move a sofa or build a deck. He was the kind of guy who wound up standing a lot when they all went out because he was the first to give up his chair. Not to mention the fact that he was a bona fide hero. When he'd gotten his commendation for his part in saving that little girl, he'd given all the credit to the rest of the team. And she hadn't missed the shine in his eyes when the Abbott family, four-year-old daughter included, had rushed in to hug him afterward.

She swallowed the lump in her throat. Did she like him?

"Yeah. I like him."

"And you're obviously attracted to him. You're both unattached and mentally sound. This was an easy sell from the beginning but now? Adding the fact that A: You know he can get you off, and B: No one else has ever been able to, including you?" She swung an imaginary bat and made a clucking sound with her mouth as if she'd knocked it out of the park. "It's a home run."

Cat's sunshine-and-rainbows view of the situation was rubbing off on her, and she managed a grin. "I guess it seems that way, huh?"

"It does. And I'm really proud of you for getting back out there. But don't forget what I said." Her tone grew serious and she waited until Courtney met her gaze. "A steamy fling should be on everyone's bucket list, so I'm behind you one hundred percent here. But don't fall in love with him, Courtney. He wasn't lying when he told you about the four-scene rule. I've never seen him with the same woman twice, besides Monica."

Courtney shoved her barely eaten bowl of salad away, her appetite completely gone. "I've heard that name twice in the past couple weeks, but never before that. What's the deal?"

Cat sighed and shook her head. "She and Rafe met in college. He was studying to be an engineer, and she wanted to teach kindergarten. It got serious fast. They dated for three years and planned to move in together after graduation."

Tears filled her friend's eyes as she paused to collect herself, and Courtney's heart plummeted to her feet. This wasn't just a bad breakup. This was something so much worse.

"She'd made a fancy dinner for Rafe on Valentine's Day and decided to run out to the liquor store to pick up a bottle of wine. There was a holdup in progress, and when she walked in and the bell jingled, the robber panicked and fired his gun. Monica took a bullet to the chest and died before the ambulance got there."

"Oh my God," Courtney whispered, her own eyes going hot. "Poor Rafe. He must have been crushed."

Cat nodded. "He dropped out of school a week later, and joined the police academy to spend his life pursuing violent criminals. His whole career is a tribute to Monica. They went to school out in Texas, so I only got to meet her a few times, but she was a sweet girl. He's never been the same. He keeps to himself a lot, and has told Shane and Galen more than once that he'll never allow himself to feel that way about another woman again." She wiped her eyes on her napkin and sucked in a deep breath. "Anyway, that's the story. I do think you can help each other in ways neither of you has even considered, but you need to be careful. I love you both, and I don't want either of you getting hurt. Promise me?"

Courtney nodded. "I promise."

"Okay." Seemingly satisfied with her answer, Cat snatched up her phone and peered down, all business again. "Now back to the survey. Is there anything you think he should know about your sexual history?"

It took Courtney longer to switch gears, and she was silent for a long moment, still thinking about Rafe and his college sweetheart. How terrible that must have been for him. No wonder he was so adamant about not getting close to anyone. She thought she had a good reason for being guarded. What she'd gone through with Wes had been a walk in the park compared to the pain Rafe had suffered.

"Courtney?"

She folded her arms to ward off the sudden chill and focused her attention back on Cat. "Sorry, what was the question?"

"Anything else about your sexual history that he should know?"

She mulled that over for a long time before shaking her head. "Nope. Nothing."

Her friend looked at her like she'd spoken in tongues. "Uhm, how's about the juicy nugget you shared with me a few minutes ago? About your ill-fated attempts to get to O-ville? Surely that's worth mentioning."

"It's pretty personal…"

"As opposed to telling him whether you like"—she glanced at the survey again—"pony play?"

She had her there. "Well, that's a specific question and has a specific answer. Besides," Courtney added with a sniff, "it would put too much pressure on him to re-create the miracle. I don't want to make him feel bad if it doesn't happen again when this is an issue I had long before him."

"Okay, if you're sure." Her reluctant shrug was enough

to make Courtney second-guess herself, but the idea of Rafe knowing that he was the first guy to ring her bell made her about break out in hives.

"I'm sure."

Cat nodded. "Okay. Looks good so far, then. Oh! We forgot to fill out number eleven on page one. What did you say your feelings were on dog leashes again?"

Courtney groaned and slumped forward to rest her head on the cool Formica while Cat huffed a sigh and called to the waitress.

"Can you grab us two coffees? And might as well keep 'em coming. I think we're going to be a while."

• • •

Nine days.

Courtney blew the lock of hair obscuring her vision from her eye and gripped the steering wheel tighter.

Nine frigging days without a single word from him. After all that fuss, all those hours of waiting, anticipating, planning...

She'd filled out the survey about hard limits and safe words; they'd exchanged medical history forms. Hell, she'd even given him a key to her house once they'd put a system in place to let him know whether or not she wanted him to use it on a given day. All that, and then?

Nada.

It was like *Indecent Proposal* without any of the indecency. Granted, she'd balked at some of the truly outrageous stuff on the questionnaire, but there was plenty left on the table to work with, and he'd seemed more than satisfied at her sense of adventure. Still, maybe it wasn't enough for him...

Whatever. She refused to let it shake her confidence. He probably decided—much like she did half the times she thought about it—that this whole thing was a terrible idea and had opted out. Fine. But it would've been nice if he'd given her a call so she could stop thinking that he'd let himself into her house and was about to ravage her every time she heard the radiator creak at night.

Which reminded her, she was going to have to ask Cat to get her key back for her. If things had been awkward before, they'd be more so now that he'd stood her up. Besides, Cat owed her one.

She adjusted her seat belt and toyed with the radio, turning back on her Rosetta Stone practice CD. It had been her lifelong dream to retire at fifty-five and travel the world, and she was hell-bent on speaking at least seven languages by that time. She'd already learned enough Spanish to eke by—especially if toilets or food were involved—and had just started on French. No way was she letting All Talk, No Action Rafe ruin her day *or* her retirement plans.

After yet another hellish forty hours at work courtesy of her new supervisor, who clearly had decided that making her life miserable was priority number one, she needed a break from the shit that had been her week. It was a beautiful summer night and she was exactly three miles from Cat's family cottage where she planned to spend a relaxing weekend by the lake. She'd been thrilled when Cat had made the offer. Courtney knew she was probably feeling a little guilty for her part in this mess. Who was she to snub the offer if it made her friend feel better?

She rolled the window down and cranked up her French lesson, letting the warm breeze batter her hair into a wild mess, not giving a crap.

"*La boulangerie*," the disembodied voice blared from the speakers. "Bakery."

"*La boulangerie*," she repeated, getting her Pepé Le Pew on, making sure to roll her tongue under to get that authentic sound working. It wasn't great, but it wasn't terrible.

She'd just turned down the dark, winding road that also acted as the Thomas family's driveway and was in the midst of learning how to order a coffee when a noise broke her concentration. An ambulance? Blue and red lights flashed in her rearview mirror, and she groaned. Cops.

"Sacre bleu!"

It was like she had the worst luck in the world in this town. First a flat and now this. She pulled to the side, glad that this time there was space to get entirely off the road. Then she turned off the radio and started digging in her glove compartment for her registration. Had she been speeding? Or maybe her blinker was on the fritz?

A flashlight blinded her, and she covered her eyes, squinting.

"Jeez, wow, that thing's pretty powerful. What's that use, nine volt there?" She tried for a smile but with her face scrunched up, she was pretty sure she'd missed the mark on looking innocent and affable and landed somewhere around weird and creepy.

"I'm going to need you to step out of the car, miss." His tone was sharp, and she winced.

"Uhm, can you tell me what I did wrong, Officer?"

The flashlight went dark and he leaned down to meet her at eye level. "I'm going to need you to step out of the car, miss. Now."

Her stomach flopped like a landed catfish as the voice registered this time. She still couldn't see well with her pupils adjusting to the lack of light again, but there was no mistake.

She raised a trembling hand to her hair and made a sad attempt to fix it as uncertainty swamped her. She'd been so bummed when he hadn't contacted her and now he was here and she wasn't sure she could go through with it. Talk about the grass being greener. "Look, Rafe, I'm not sure—"

"This is your last warning. Step out of the car, or I will forcibly remove you from it."

The icy command jarred her into action, and she reached for the door handle. With a yank, she opened it and stepped onto the grass. How familiar this part felt. They were only a few miles from where they'd had their last encounter, and her body seemed to recognize that fact. Her nipples stiffened beneath her tank top under the warm breeze and her pulse skittered wildly.

She could see him now. He was decked out in his dress blues, baton at his hip, gun on his belt. Delicious. His dark eyes were so intense her arms broke out in goose bumps in spite of the warm evening.

"Do you have any weapons?" he asked curtly.

She shook her head. "What? No."

"Put your hands on the roof of the car."

"I'm sure this isn't ne—"

"Ma'am, unless you want to find yourself down at County, put your hands on the fucking roof and spread 'em."

It was that last part that had her actually considering his request. She knew for a fact she was the only one coming to the cottage this weekend, and there were no other houses down this stretch of "road," but what if someone made a wrong turn? Unlikely, considering how few cars came up that way, but possible. Before she'd made up her mind, she found herself spread-eagled and cuffed without ceremony. Jesus he was fast.

"Rafe..."

"Listen to me carefully, ma'am, because I'm only going to say this once. I'm going to give you instructions, and you're going to follow them."

The precariousness of her position made the butterflies in her belly start flapping. The form he'd had her fill out included a space for her safe word. She had chosen a two word phrase instead. Toy boat. She could "toy boat" him right now and this would all stop. The scene would end.

"Do you understand?"

She nodded slowly. "Yes, Officer."

He let out a sigh and cleared his throat. "Good."

She tried to stay still as he frisked her, but it was impossible. He wasn't gentle. There was no hesitation. He ran his hands up her bare leg from ankle to thigh and down the other, and then between, lingering long enough that she would have filed a lawsuit if this were real. But it wasn't. So why not have a little fun?

She worked up her courage and tried to keep her voice steady. "Officer, is that standard?"

Her back talk got her a second squeeze through her jean shorts, and she couldn't stop herself from flexing into his hand.

"What do we have here?" he muttered.

"I can assure you that's not a weapon, sir," she said, already hearing the edge of need working its way into her voice.

He released her and slid both hands over her hips, past her rib cage and up until he cupped both of her breasts. Her nipples stood at attention, and he grunted in approval, pinching them lightly before releasing her and stepping back.

"I'm not a hard man by nature," he said, fingering the links of the cuffs around her wrists lightly. "But I can be, if I'm not happy." He closed the circle more tightly, two clicks, until the metal dug into her skin. "We can both walk away from this unfortunate incident happy tonight."

She shuddered at the sternness of his tone, laced with precisely enough sensual promise to temper fear with desire.

"H-how?" And she so wanted to know. As much as she'd enjoyed their first encounter, it had gone against the grain for her to take and not give something in return. It had been bothering her ever since. A low-level annoyance that never really went away. But she had the chance to fix that now.

He didn't answer her question. Instead, he took her by the shoulders and turned her to face him. By the light of the moon, she could make out the pulse pounding in his neck, and it gave her courage.

She stepped toward him, ignoring the twinge in her wrists as she moved.

"Get on your knees," he ground out.

She paused and cocked her head at him. Was he serious? She tried to read his unfathomable eyes, but came up empty. She was supposed to drop down and go to town or…?

"I'm a busy man, miss. Lots of bad people running around and not a lot of time to catch them. Either you can suck me off or we can put that sweet ass in the back of my car and you can spend the night in jail. Your call."

Blood pounded in her ears, and, to her surprise, between her legs at the harshness of his voice…the crassness of his words.

She sank slowly down, reveling in the pained expression on his face. Like he wanted her so badly, he could hardly stand it. Like her kneeling pleased him so much, he could barely contain it. *Magnifique*. She kept her eyes locked on him as her knees touched the cool, soft grass.

"What now?"

• • •

Great question.

His brain was scrambled ten ways to Sunday, but he was supposed to know. It was his job to lead her, teach her, guide her, and he wasn't going to let the fact that she continually blew his mind distract him from that task. Her wide eyes stared up at him, glassy with need. He'd been pretty sure she would like this scene.

In spite of her hesitance to fill it out, the survey had been very telling, and he was thrilled to see that most of the things she seemed enthusiastic about were a great match for his own tastes.

Her tongue poked out and wet her lips, and suddenly he was done thinking, opting instead just to feel. And right now, he wanted nothing more than to feel that mouth on him. His cock bucked behind his zipper, and he made quick work of his belt before yanking his pants apart. Her gaze shot down to watch him with rapt attention as he freed his throbbing erection from his boxers.

"Open," he barked sharply, hot blood coursing through his veins when she complied without question. He couldn't help but stop to enjoy the view for a few seconds. Courtney, head back, the skin of her throat bared to him as she waited for him to slide his cock between those soft lips. The ache became too much, and he stroked himself hard once, gripping his shaft and working up to the sensitive head.

Her breath went choppy and she swayed toward him, like a willow in the wind. Her tongue darted out again and she leaned in farther. She wanted it. Wanted his cock in her mouth. Wanted to suck him off until he came. The knowledge made him dizzy with need.

He'd been with women who didn't like sucking dick. He'd been with women who didn't mind it, and he'd been with women who liked it, especially because it pleased him. But he'd yet to find a woman who loved it for the sake of loving it. If Courtney was that woman…

With a hiss, he gripped the back of her head and fed his cock into her hot, waiting mouth. She wasted no time, moaning low in her throat, drawing him in hard and deep. He let his eyes drift shut for a second, and lights exploded behind his lids as she leaned away to lap delicately at the aching head.

She moaned again when a drop of come leaked out and then tipped her head to catch it with her tongue.

"Fu-uck," he groaned, spearing his hand through her long hair, using his hold to work her over him, slow first and then faster. She opened, pulling him down into the column of her throat until he reached bottom, and still she dove forward for more, consuming him, swallowing him whole.

The need to come hit him like a prizefighter, making his solar plexus clench, making his balls pull up tight, locked and ready for launch. Too soon. Way too fucking soon. He had a promise to keep and while he was good with his hands, and even better with his mouth, he needed to feel that pussy clenching over him when she came.

He tugged her hair softly at first, then harder, but she didn't release him. She whimpered low in her throat, and he couldn't stop himself from caving to her sensual, wordless demand for more.

He flexed hard, driving his cock farther, harder. She gagged, her throat clenching around him, and he let go of her head instantly, and waited for her to back away. Instead, she dropped low again, deep-throating him until he battered the tender flesh at the back of her throat again and again.

"Enough," he bit out, even as his hands drifted back to her hair. Even as he traced the concave hollow of her cheeks as she did her level best to suck him dry.

The point of no return was so close, he could see the finish line, and if he didn't stop her now, there would be no stopping until he exploded into her hot mouth.

He gripped her head firmly with one hand and tapped her sharply on the jaw with the other. She met his gaze with dazed eyes, in the grip of a sexual frenzy that killed him to interrupt.

"That's enough."

She blinked blearily up at him and nodded, then settled

back on her heels, ragged breaths racking her body.

"Y-you said I had to suck you off," she whispered, eyes drifting back to his dick.

"And now I've changed my mind."

"Did I not do a good job? My ex said it's slutty to do that and—"

"I stopped you because I need to be inside you. And your ex is clearly the stupidest motherfucker to ever own a dick if he didn't like that."

Her cheeks flushed, and she gave him a smile that made his heart squeeze.

"His...ah, wasn't quite that..." She eyed him again and licked her lips.

If a man could die of horniness, he would have expired on the spot. For all her big talk about what she was into and what she wasn't, this woman was a fucking dream.

"Stand up," he demanded, taking her arm to help her. It was slow going, and he realized she was still shaking.

His intention had been to fuck her like he'd said he was going to, but plans changed the second he saw her standing there, long, trim legs spread wide, nipples poking out against the thin cotton of her shirt. He stepped close, his cock throbbing in time with his heartbeat.

Reaching into his pocket, he withdrew the key to the cuffs. "Turn around."

She did, and he slid the key into the lock and released her before turning her to face him again.

"Until our business is concluded here, you're still the prisoner, but I want your hands free. Do you know why?"

She shook her head slowly, rubbing at the pink marks on her wrist.

"So you can use them to hold on to me while I eat your pussy until you come all over my tongue," he explained, his voice more rasp than anything. He watched her closely to see how she reacted to his language, and when her nostrils flared lightly and a shiver ran through her, a surge of satisfaction tore through him. She couldn't be more perfect if she'd been made especially for him. They were sexual C-4 together.

Without another word, he reached for her shorts. They were blessedly easy to maneuver, no buttons or zippers to contend with as he yanked them to her ankles along with her underwear. He knew she was ready, knew she was hot for him, so he didn't bother with niceties. He just knelt and set his mouth on her.

"Jesus, Rafe," she cried, her fingers lacing into his hair just as he'd predicted. He tried to take his time, tried to stop from consuming her, but the scent, the taste of her, jacked his need up to an eleven. Working her swollen clit mercilessly with his tongue, he circled his arms around her, clutching her firm ass, sealing her to his face.

She spread her legs farther apart on a wordless cry and he used the space to get in deeper…to close the very edge of his teeth gently around that sensitive bundle of nerves to hold in place, and then he sucked, hard.

The hands in his hair convulsed, yanking as she screamed his name over and over. She twitched and jerked and still he worked her, her wild, uninhibited response making him insatiable.

"Inside me," she cried. "Please."

He barely heard her over the pounding in his ears, but there was no mistaking the pressure of her hands in his hair as she urged him up.

With a silent thanks to the fertility gods that she was on the pill, he hoisted her up into his arms and sat her on the hood of the car. She kicked off her shorts and leaned back on her elbows, thighs spread. "I wanna see," she said softly, and her already-flushed cheeks went pinker.

"Oh, me too, cupcake."

He took his cock in hand and moved between her thighs, groaning when the head came into contact with her slick, soaking-wet pussy. She stared down at him, lips parted, as he slid into her waiting heat. It was a tight fit, tight enough that he gritted his teeth from the effort of trying not to come.

"You feel so good," she murmured, her eyes fluttering closed, rolling her hips into him in a circular motion that looked as sexy as it felt. He gave her more, pushing deeper until she gasped.

"God, that's—" She broke off, her throat working as she swallowed.

"More?" he growled. She nodded and every nerve ending screamed with the need to finish it. He didn't hold back this time, letting it loose, plunging hard and deep, until his balls were flush with her ass. His body quaked as the orgasm sang to him, a siren's song, tugging him closer.

God, he hoped she was close again. He took one, experimental thrust, a long stroke that pulled almost all the way out before sliding all the way back in. The friction was so sublime it nearly ended him.

With a low groan, he slid one hand between her thighs and thumbed her clit as he began to fuck her in earnest, driving forward and back in a relentless rhythm. She sat up then, wrapping her arms and legs around him, working her hips in a frantic dance against his.

"Oh, God," she murmured once, and then again. A second later she froze, her legs gripping his waist like iron bars as she exploded around him. His brain short-circuited and his hips took over, pounding faster as her pussy clenched over him, milking him like a hot little fist. He shouted her name as the climax ripped through him. Cock pulsing and jerking, he exploded.

It seemed like forever but was probably only a few minutes before his heartbeat finally returned to normal and he had the strength to disengage from her clutches.

Now came the tricky part. What he wanted was to follow her the rest of the way down this road and spend the weekend doing exactly what they'd just done and more, over and over. Out of the question. Not just because he had to meet an informant later tonight, but also because they had a deal. For the first time since he'd implemented the four-scene rule five years before, it didn't seem like enough. The fact that he'd had to wait so long for her was obviously fucking with his head. Celibacy would do that to a man. After the next scene, he'd be able to see things more clearly.

"You okay?" he asked.

She opened her eyes and nodded. "I'm great."

Great was very good. He patted her thigh gently and tucked himself back into his pants as she stood, tugging her shorts on. Wasn't often he wore his dress blues, but she seemed to like them. He filed that information away for possible future use.

"Listen, I'm sorry I didn't get in touch sooner. I caught a tricky case at work and spent all of my days and most of my nights at the precinct or out in the field. I wanted to make sure we did this right."

That was the truth. He had considered calling, but that would've crossed the line between a purely sexual contract to something a man would have done with his girlfriend. He didn't break a date or change plans, he just had taken longer to implement them.

"It's fine. I wasn't sure if you'd changed you mind or…"

"Oh, definitely not that." Her smile spurred him on and the words were out before he could stop them. "Are you meeting everyone at the carnival Sunday night? Galen and Lacey will be back from Puerto Rico, so it should be fun."

She hesitated and his stomach cramped. What the hell had he brought that up for? This was his first time doing a scene with someone who was also a friend of sorts, and he was cursing himself for blurring the lines between the two.

"I was thinking about it," she said before he could figure a way to backtrack. "Are we…doing that? I wasn't sure if we were supposed to avoid each other socially until our business had concluded or not."

The idea didn't seem to concern her either way; she looked more perplexed than anything. No point in making a mountain out of a molehill, then. Besides, keeping things as normal as possible would make the transition back to the usual easier on everyone.

"Fried food, balloon animals, and rickety-ass roller coaster? Where else would I be?"

She ran a hand through her mussed hair. "Okay, I guess I'll see you there, then."

The response made him way happier than it should have. He stalked back to his car, more determined than ever to focus on their next scene. In fact, it wasn't like a date, so maybe he'd skip the carnival altogether.

The little voice he was determined to ignore spoke again, a single word this time.

Liar.

Chapter Six

Courtney stared in the mirror, filled with the sort of loathing usually reserved for family holidays and orifice-doctor visits. After five outfits, three hairstyles, and six shoe changes, she was no closer to being ready for the carnival than she'd been when she started.

There was no reason for things to be so complicated. None. This wasn't even a date. It was like old times, nobody to impress, same as ever. The group hanging out.

No big deal.

Mostly.

No matter how hard she tried to convince herself otherwise, everything was different, and no matter how many outfits she tried on, there was no way around the fact that she felt completely naked.

She grabbed for her cell phone and shot a quick message to Cat, letting her know she'd be running late. The carnival on the far side of town was only twenty minutes away, but at this rate, she wouldn't be ready until it came around next year.

With a long-suffering sigh, she pulled on her favorite capri-length skinny jeans, a kitschy off-the-shoulder shirt with a graphic of Marilyn Monroe on it, and a pair of strappy sandals that weren't as high as she liked, but were plenty high enough for walking around the carnival grounds all night. Staring at herself in the mirror, she fluffed out her hair. It didn't look too "try hard," but she didn't look like something the cat dragged in either. Not bad.

Before she had time to rethink her outfit yet again, she snatched her phone and bag and dashed out the door, refusing to give the mirror one more glance as she passed it. She climbed into her car and sped down the road, repeating over and over to herself what a good idea it would be to get out of the house. And to see her friends.

One of whom is Rafe.

Which reminded her, Lacey had called yesterday the second she'd gotten in from the airport. She'd wanted to tell Courtney in person, but couldn't wait. She and Galen were adopting a baby girl. They'd gotten word while they were away, and Lacey was ecstatic. She'd known for over a year now that conception would be near impossible, and after some rough patches, things had finally fallen into place.

Because she and Galen were busy painting the nursery and baby-proofing the house, they weren't going to make it tonight. It was a bummer, but at least Cat and Shane would be there. Not only did she want to see them both, she also needed a buffer from the Costco-sized vat of awkwardness that was sure to accompany her and Rafe's first post-sex encounter.

No big deal, she reminded herself. *Mostly.*

She parked in the grassy field outside the fairgrounds and walked toward the entry gate where Cat and Shane had told her to meet them. She searched high and low for her friend's trademark fiery red hair, but there was no sign of her.

What she did recognize was the towering wall of muscle topped off with a beautiful face, featuring dark eyes that seemed to look right through her.

Rafe.

She plucked at her shirt and took a deep breath. If she kept touching her clothes, maybe it would help her remember that even though he was looking at her like she was naked, she wasn't actually nude.

Maybe.

It'd be fine. The others would be here in five minutes tops and then it would all go back to normal.

"Hey, Courtney."

Why did he insist on saying her name like that? Like he was even giving the syllables oral or something.

"Nice shirt," he said, his gaze skimming over her figure and leaving a trail of fire in its path.

"Hey. Where is everybody?" She ignored his last comment and focused instead on hitching her purse up on her shoulder. With a deep breath, she willed herself to meet his stare. Mistake. If she didn't feel naked before, she sure as hell did now. The worst part of it all was that she wasn't sure whether she wanted to cross her arms over her chest or stretch them above her head so he could get the full view.

"Cat just texted me. Didn't she tell you? They're not coming. Some kind of work thing came up."

Nerves made her throat go instantly dry, and she swallowed hard. *Some kind of work thing*, huh? Sounded really important. She made an internal note to murder Cat.

"Interesting. Galen and Lacey can't make it either."

They stared at each other in silence. What now? Surely this broke all the rules they'd set from the start. Her stomach twisted as she thought over her options. She could go in with him and eat enough funnel cake to get herself seriously ill so she could leave. Or, she could create a superhero alter ego and say that she was needed back at the lair ASAP to meet up with her sidekick, or the city was doomed.

"Are you coming or what?" He was a yard away from her, his body twisted in a way that highlighted his incredible jawline and the way his jeans clung to his powerful thighs. God help her. Even in the horrendous carnival lighting, he looked like something out of a fitness magazine.

Decisions, decisions. "I, uh—"

He crossed the space between them in an instant, grasping her wrist before she had time to acknowledge the contact. "Look, it's not like either of us planned this. What would we have done a month ago in this situation?"

"Nothing, I guess. Hung out at the carnival, maybe."

He raised his dark brows and eyed her, and she pulled at her T-shirt with her free hand. The sheer electricity of his presence had her heart thumping in overtime. How was she supposed to handle an entire evening like this? Four scenes was one thing. Pure fantasy, never to cross over into reality. A date, intentional or not, was something else entirely.

"Look, we had a deal. I don't want to mess it up. Or something." She mentally gave herself a high five for eloquence. She was nothing if not articulate.

His lips quirked in a crooked smile, and he led her toward the entrance. "Let's not put more on this than there has to be. It's a night at the carnival between friends, not a proposal, okay?"

Maybe it was his freakish height. Or the mind-melding power of his gaze. She couldn't pinpoint why. All she knew was that she nodded her agreement before the rest of her body had time to weigh in on a decision. Within minutes, they were strolling through the grounds, marveling over the assortment of weird food carts.

"Tempura-fried Twix bars with bacon bits?" He pointed to a stand where a small rotund man was passing out carton after carton of greasy goodness or grossness, depending upon a person's preference. "We have to try that."

"I think I'll pass, thanks." She scrunched up her nose and he laughed, flashing his brilliantly white smile. God, there had to be one thing about him for her to focus on to get through the rest of the night. Couldn't his nose have been crooked at least, or his shoulders not broad enough? Something, anything, to distract her from the fact that he looked like he'd fallen out of the sky in search of his hammer.

"Suit yourself." He shrugged and walked ahead, the back side of him reminding her that yes, he was perfect from that angle as well. Frustrating.

She had to find something to distract herself. Something for them to do. Something for her to think about besides how warm his hand had felt around her wrist.

"Hey, you wanna play a game?" She stopped short, looking around to take stock of where she was. There were rows of carnival games on either side of them—balloon darts, water guns, goldfish—all the classics. One of the attractions was sure to grab his attention.

"Which prize do you want?" he asked, one of his signature cocky smiles already splitting his face.

"What makes you so sure you can win?" She grinned in spite of herself. And why not? They were friends. Sort of. People had fun with their friends.

The grin threatened to morph into semi-hysterical laughter for a second before she got hold of herself again.

"I'm an expert at carnival games."

She rolled her eyes and gestured toward the goldfish. "I think I can win a fish by myself."

"And if you can't? What do I get?"

A familiar sense of terror and excitement spread through her, and she found herself backing away, her hands held up in surrender. "Oh no, I've already been to this rodeo. I'm not going there."

"Come on, what are you, chicken?" He was baiting her, and she'd be stupid to fall for it. And yet, his words dug at her. She lowered her hands and planted them on her hips, eyeing him.

"I'm not chicken. I just have a code that precludes me from taking on two dares at once," she lied.

"We'll make it super low stakes, then. How about if you don't win a fish for yourself and I win one for you, then you have to ride the Ferris wheel with me."

Her fear of heights was legendary. She got scared when she jumped a little too high. And still…she'd promised herself that her time with Rafe would be pure fantasy. A break from reality. A way to stretch her wings, face her fears, and gain back some of the confidence she'd lost. No reason for her not to stick to that part of the plan, even if tonight hadn't exactly been part of their arrangement.

"You've got a deal."

She sidled up to the little red booth and dug her feet in like a pitcher on the mound. This was for more than a pet with a four-day life span. This was for honor. For glory. For women who were afraid of heights everywhere.

She slapped her money on the counter and had half a mind to spit on the ground like a baseball pro. Instead, she tossed Rafe what she hoped was a saucy smirk and he had the courtesy to look entirely unimpressed. Whatever. The proof would be in the pudding.

The carnie sat three ping-pong balls in front of her and she nodded to him in thanks.

"Are you ready to see how a pro does it?" she asked.

"Is someone going before you?" He laughed at his own joke and she wound up, pitching the ball clean over all of the goldfish bowls until it landed on the other side of the booth, on the grass, with a little plop. A kid around the age of five picked it up and tossed it back into the game, landing the ball directly in one of the bowls.

"Mommy, look," he said, "I did it."

His mother pulled him along, her lids already half-closed in exhaustion.

"That counts," Courtney said earnestly.

"Like. Hell."

She abandoned her attempt at swaying Rafe and leveled a wide-eyed pout at the carnie in a bid for sympathy, but he only laughed and shook his head. Men. They always stuck together.

"It's fine. I was just warming up. Sometimes I'm too powerful for my own good."

She licked her forefinger to test the wind and then tossed the second ball. It landed squarely in the middle of the group of fish bowls, but it landed in none of them.

"Do you want me to blow really hard and see if it moves?" he goaded.

"Nope." Now she was bound and determined. She ground her feet into the grass, practicing the arc of her throw a few times, mentally cuing up the theme from *Rocky* for inspiration. "It's all in the follow-through."

"I've heard that," Rafe said on a probably fake yawn.

"You'll see." She narrowed her eyes at him and flicked her wrist.

In fact, she flicked her wrist so hard that the ball landed directly behind her in the grass.

"Wow, you got me there. I did not see that one coming."

She scrambled for the ball, but he snatched it from her before her fingers made contact.

"Let me show you how a *real* pro does it."

He assumed the position, and just as he was about to make his move, she shouted, "Wait! Behind the back. Double or nothing."

Ha. Let him try that. There was no way he'd—
Plunk.

She wasn't sure whether the sound was from the ball connecting with the water in the fishbowl or if it was simply the sound of her heart dropping into her stomach. Without pausing to even eyeball the distance, he'd turned and sunk the ball in the nearest bowl, no questions asked. A perfect shot.

"I thought I'd save you the humiliation of continuing." He winked at her and took the goldfish from the carnie. "Now you just have to decide what to name him. Personally, I like Gil. Seems a good name for a fish."

"Were you always like this and I just never noticed?" she asked, sprinting to meet up with him in the line for tickets.

"Charming? Witty?"

Exactly. She'd seen him interact with the others in the group that way, with jokes and lighthearted banter, but between them, things always felt heavy and tense. This was the first time she'd been on the receiving end of this side of Rafe, and she was liking it far more than she should have. Not that she was about to tell him that.

"Irritating."

"Yes." He exchanged his money with the teller at the window and sauntered away, already making a beeline for the Ferris wheel. "But your insults won't distract me. Come on, chicken."

She hung back for a moment to pull herself together. *Deep, soothing breaths,* she reminded herself. Instead of facing one fear tonight, she was going to face them all. At once.

And the first of them was already standing in line for the ride, motioning for her to join him.

Just. Freaking. Perfect.

• • •

From the moment the "wheel of death," as Courtney had coined it, cranked into motion, it had been his prime objective to ensure she didn't die by way of panic attack. With every inch the ride moved up into the air, she was edging closer to the handrail, obviously trying to hide the fact that she was gripping it so hard her knuckles had turned white. "*Merde*," she muttered under her breath.

He paused and turned to face her. "You speak French?"

Her cheeks stayed pasty and she didn't look his way. "No. I mean, not really. I like languages so I try to learn them in my spare time."

"All of them?" he asked incredulously.

"Ideally. But I'm gunning for at least seven over the next twenty-five years."

He resisted the urge to smile at that nugget of information because, in spite of his attempts to distract her, she was still focused entirely on the safety bar in front of them.

"Have you seriously never ridden the Ferris wheel before?"

"Listen, maybe you go skeet shooting, and, I don't know, BASE jumping all the time, but not all of us are risk takers like that." She forced a laugh that ended up sounding a lot more like a whimper.

He realized very quickly that the time for jokes had passed. She was really scared. He wanted to kick himself for dragging her onto the ride. "Hey, look at me. You're going to be fine." He reached out and tucked his fingers beneath her chin, pulling her attention toward him. For a moment, she still focused intently on the ground, but in the next, their gazes met. He had half an urge to pull his hand back, almost singed by the electricity that sizzled between them in that instant, but he resisted.

Instead, he cupped her jaw, catching a few strands of her hair in his caress. "You're okay," he murmured.

She nodded and slid away from the railing, leaning into his touch. Their knees brushed in the tin-can-size seats, and then he was gliding his hand around her neck, stroking her nape, stock-still as she moved closer to touch her soft mouth to his. She groaned, pressing more heavily into him, curling her arms around his neck.

God, she smelled good. Sweet, like peaches. He slipped his tongue between her lips, tasting her. She responded instantly, crushing her breasts against him, kissing him back with everything she had. What had started out as a gesture meant to comfort turned on a dime, and he growled low in his throat, need pulsing through him in waves.

When the ride suddenly cranked to a halt, it was far too soon. He was still in a daze when he realized they were at the bottom and it was their turn to exit. Courtney bolted so quick that he was amazed she didn't leave a trail of dust behind her. He eased his way out, carrying her goldfish in front of him, strategically using poor Gil to camouflage his erection.

When he finally saw her standing in the crowd, she would barely meet his gaze. Instead, she tugged on her T-shirt, staring intently at the ground.

He'd really fucked this up bad. She may have been the one to kiss him, but he'd made her a deal. Four scenes. No strings. It wasn't just for her sake. It was for both of them. The reason they made so much sense on paper was because they had great sexual chemistry, but no interest in falling in love. Her, not now. Him, not ever again.

The thought strengthened his resolve and he approached her cautiously. Lovers three more times, and friends from here on out. That was the plan.

"Hey, you lived," he said, striving to recapture the earlier light mood of the evening.

She gave him half a smile, her lashes still shading her eyes from his view. "It would seem that way."

"You look disappointed. The only solution to that is the tempura-fried candy bar, I think."

"Yeah, that should do me in for sure."

"That or if you tried one of the dart games. With your aim, you might impale yourself."

She let out a genuine laugh, and he coaxed her into one more stroll around the grounds. After sampling more food than they should have, including chocolate-covered bacon, they stumbled out into the parking lot, stomachs filled to bursting. With every step they took, the lights grew dimmer behind them, and by the time he'd reached the row where they'd both parked, it was mostly dark.

He paused in front of her car, and they both started talking at the same time. He stopped, and waited for her to continue.

"Hey, I know it was—" She cleared her throat and shook out her hair behind her. "Kind of weird at first, but I want you to know that I had a really good time tonight. I'm, um, I'm glad I didn't bail after the Ferris wheel."

"Yeah, it was a lot of fun." They stood in silence for a moment, surveying each other. Finally he broke the tension. "Look, that was no big deal. The kiss. Chalk it up to fear and adrenaline, okay?"

"For sure." She nodded so vigorously that he was sure her head would hurt the next day. "Sounds good." She darted to the driver's-side door of her car, only to come scurrying back before he'd taken a single step.

"I forgot Gil." She held out her hand for the fish.

"Right, right." He nodded and handed it over. She met his gaze for another heart-pounding minute before getting into her car and cranking the engine.

He waited until she pulled out before walking slowly

to his own car. What the hell had gotten into him? He'd let the simple fun of the night and the pleasant company addle his senses and make him act like a high school quarterback with a crush on the head cheerleader. The sooner he put a stop to that shit, the better, before he really botched it all up. He'd promised Courtney an introduction to BDSM and the chance to explore her sexuality with him, and he was going to deliver. But that and his friendship were all he had to give. He needed to make sure that neither of them forgot that.

Now he needed to regain the ground he'd lost ASAP and make sure there was no confusion lingering for either one of them. Time to get back to basics.

Chapter Seven

Time to make her move. With the *Mission: Impossible* theme song playing in her head, Courtney glanced up and down the long hospital corridor before scurrying to the bank of elevators. Keeping a watchful eye, she thumped the down button repeatedly, a silent prayer on auto-loop in her head. When the arrow lit green, she blew out the breath she'd been holding.

Almost home free.

After the way things had ended between her and Rafe, she'd considered calling out from work that morning. She'd spent half the night tossing and turning. It was only the thought of sitting at home with way too much time to think about this thing with him that made her bite the bullet and don her scrubs. By the time it was over ten endless hours later, she was regretting that decision heartily.

Work had been brutal. Three stabbings—those always increased in the summer as heat made people stabby— and a three-car pileup on the interstate that had been a veritable blood bath. One person had died on the scene but the team of ER doctors had managed to keep the fatalities to the one. That was a blessing.

What hadn't been a blessing was when her asshole supervisor Barry had asked her to stay two hours past her shift to straighten out paperwork that wasn't even hers. The guy had been at the hospital for all of three months and had been a holy terror, screaming at the nurses and taking advantage of them all by piling on double shifts with total disregard to their home lives. It was getting to be a major issue. One that was starting to make Courtney hate a job she used to love and had her sneaking around like a thief in the night in hopes of avoiding him in case he found yet another reason for her to stay longer.

By the time she slogged her way up the winding path to her front door, she could think of nothing besides sipping on a sizable glass of cheap wine snuggled beneath her down comforter with the air-conditioner blasting in her face while she read a sexy novel.

Paradise.

Her weary muscles protested as she trudged up the stairs, tugging off her scrubs as she went. When she reached her bedroom and flicked on the light, weariness fled to make way for an almost dizzying wave of excitement.

On her bed sat a large rectangular box. Pristine white with a red envelope resting on the lid, but otherwise unadorned. It was stupid, really, but the breath caught in her throat just looking at it, so beautiful in its simplicity, so civilized and elegant, which was such a contrast to what was likely inside.

This was it. Scene number two.

Part of her was a tiny bit disappointed. When they'd sussed out the details of their arrangement and she'd agreed to give him her house key, he'd given her two scarves. One red and one green. If she preferred he not use the key on a given day, she was to tie the red one on her balcony. If she was open to him letting himself in for a scene, she should use the green one. She'd gone with red the first few nights out of nervousness, but when she hadn't heard from him, she'd gone green and had left it that way ever since. Many a night was spent tossing and turning, fantasizing about waking up with his magical mouth on her.

But the disappointment faded fast as she inched toward her bed, excitement building with every step. She refused to credit her now-shaking legs to bone-deep relief that there was going to be a scene two at all after the way they'd ended. She was sure she'd blown it when she kissed him, but now here he was. A strange sensation settled over her. Happiness that he wanted more time with her was mixed with fear that every minute she spent with him, she was skating closer and closer to trouble.

He'd been hard to resist when he was one-dimensional— controlled dom Rafe, who held the power to make her tremble in his fingertips. Now that she'd gotten to sample the other side of him? The funny, sweet guy who'd held her when she was afraid on the Ferris wheel and won her a pet goldfish? He was lethal.

But even as fear and doubt clouded her mind, she never considered walking away and leaving the box unopened. She had three more nights with him, and short of an apocalypse, she wasn't giving them up for anything or anyone. She'd push on and deal with the fallout when it was over.

Her fingers shook with a combination of nerves and anticipation as she picked up the envelope. With a steadying breath, she tore it open with a singular swipe of her thumb. The paper was typed on high-end card stock that was like silk under her fingertips. She read the lines once, willing the thudding of her heart to slow, then again, trying to process all of his instructions.

Courtney—

Meet me at the Feldmoore Hotel on Edgemont Street at 7 p.m. Ask the concierge for a key to Mr. Welter's room at the front desk.

You are to wear nothing except the contents of this box, and your hair should be up.

When you enter the room, go straight to the safe on the west wall and open it. The code is 41-42-69.

Do *not* be late.

Rafe

Her breath was coming in short bursts as she wrenched open the package, peeling back the crimson tissue paper to reveal its contents. A sleek black trench coat with leather leggings to match and a pair of black stilettos stared up at her. Searching for the shirt to complete the outfit, she riffled through all the tissue until it sat in a pile on the carpet, but turned up nada.

No top, which was surely no accident. Rafe was meticulous, focused, and detail-oriented. If he'd wanted her to wear a top, it would've been in the box.

She chewed on her bottom lip and surveyed the instructions a second time before glancing at the clock. Six twenty. The Feldmoore was twenty minutes away, and if she was going to make it there on time, she'd have to leave ASAP. Her hands shook with excitement as she set the letter down and headed into the bathroom. She stripped the rest of her clothes off and took a shower so fast that Guinness himself would've applauded.

Wasting no time, she tugged on a thong and the leather

leggings, hopping up and down until the dastardly snug material cleared her ass to rest low on her hips. She reached around to hook her bra, then shook her head. Surely he hadn't meant that she couldn't wear her bra. She already didn't have a shirt.

Weighing her options, she shrugged off the lacy cups and slung the coat over her shoulders before fastening the belt and slipping into the stilettos. She took one quick second to admire them and nodded approvingly.

By the time she pulled up to the hotel and handed off the keys to the valet, it was six fifty-five. The humid breeze was a potent reminder that she was dressed in leather and a trench coat in the heat of summer. That combined with the weight of her nerves had her beyond frazzled and by the time she reached the concierge desk, she was sure her heart was close to exploding in her chest.

She cleared her throat and some unknown force pried the question from her lips. "Hello, um, could you please tell me which room Mr., uh, Welter's room is? By any chance?" Her cheeks boiled, but the concierge smiled and slid a key across the desk to her without question.

"Two-oh-six. Second floor. The elevator is on your right, madam." He gestured toward the glass lift and she nodded, clacking her way toward it without another word.

When she got to the room, she paused outside the doorway. Her palms were slick with sweat as she laid a hand on the knob and mustered up her courage.

Now or never. Fight or flight, at it again.

She slid the key in, and the door clicked open. Her breath caught along with it and she stepped into the room, heart hammering. Once inside, all her fears took a backseat, crowded out by her primary objective. Her instructions were to go straight to the safe and open it, so that was what she'd do. Whatever happened after that…well, that was what had her thighs shaking and her mouth going dry.

The room was pitch dark, and with a hesitant finger she reached out to tap the light on. The only source was a crystal chandelier that shone dimly over the wide, satin-covered bed. The space was warm and lavish, an unlit fireplace on the far side of the room with champagne chilling in a bucket of ice by a side table. A couple of chairs nestled close by the hearth.

And a safe, sitting unprotected near the wide oak wardrobe.

Her pulse bucked hard in time with every footfall, but she moved as quietly as possible. When she reached the wall, she dropped to her knees and entered the pass code she'd memorized. The lock tumbled beneath her fingertips and the door swung open.

Well, that was easy. She peered into the safe wishing she'd thought to bring a flashlight, but before she could get a look at the contents, she felt a tug on her ponytail. Soft at first and then with growing pressure as it was used to pull her to standing. A vise gripped her chest, and it was suddenly a struggle to breathe.

"Here to steal from me, are you?" Rafe's voice was a low rumble, the thunder before a lightning strike, and she didn't know whether to be relieved or even more nervous.

"What? You told me to—" She caught herself. Ah, so this was the game—she was a thief, and he her mark—and she was supposed to play it. It wasn't hard to imagine. The man before her was a one-eighty from the man who had fed her cotton candy and kissed her on the Ferris wheel the night before.

One hand was still firmly gripping her hair, but the other had snaked toward her trench coat, pulling her back, flush against the hard, muscled expanse of his chest. Her voice was breathier than she would've liked when she spoke again. "I'm certain I don't know what you're talking about, and I'd appreciate it if you released me at once."

His laugh was short and mirthless, sending a frisson of fear through her even as heat collected between her thighs. Damn, he was good at this.

"You think because you've got a pretty face and nice tits that I'm going to let you walk away? Sorry, that's not the way I do business." He shoved her toward the bed and she landed heavily on the silken mattress. If it hurt, she didn't notice. She was too filled with roiling emotions, each competing for center stage. Fear, curiosity, and—to her chagrin—undeniable lust, almost vicious in its intensity.

She twisted to face him. He towered over her, black pants fitted to enhance the appearance of his strong thighs, chest perfectly contoured beneath a tailored white shirt. A wall of stone. Unbreakable.

His smile in the dim light was chilling as he stared down at her. He didn't break eye contact as he raised a hand to deftly remove one cufflink and then the other, speaking while he worked. "If you were a man in my position, Miss…?" He raised his brows questioningly.

She racked her brain to supply a name despite the riot going on inside her and spit out the first thing that came to mind. "M-Mary. Mary Mack."

Her heart tripped when his eyes twinkled, a grin tugging at his lips. She squinted, confused by the sudden change in his demeanor. Then she glanced down at her clothes.

Yup, good old Miss Mary Mack.

All dressed in black.

Her cheeks burned with humiliation as she scrambled into a seated position. Only her second try and she was officially the worst temporary submissive in history. Would he call the whole thing off now that she'd effectively dumped a pitcher of ice water on their steamy start with her unintentional silliness?

To Rafe's credit, and her everlasting relief, his eyes went flat in an instant, and ruthless Mr. Welter was back. "Do you take me for a fool, Ms. Mack? Plucking your alias from a child's nursery rhyme. Do I look like a man to be trifled with?"

He prowled back and forth at the foot of the bed, never taking his gaze off her as he meticulously rolled each of his sleeves to expose his thick, muscular forearms. She swallowed hard, straightening her posture to meet his gaze head-on.

"Honestly?" She let her gaze trip over his body lightly and then shrugged. "You look pretty much the same as any other man to me." She punctuated that with a cheeky wink. "Sorry to disappoint."

Well, hot damn, Mary Mack was a firecracker, and apparently, Courtney wasn't the only one who thought so. A grudging respect lit her captor's face and she felt his approval from head to toe. Like she'd been out in the cold and suddenly found herself basking under the rays of the sun.

"Oh, I doubt you'll disappoint. While I might look like other men to you, I can assure you that's far from the case, and the thought that I might allow you to fail me is one I wouldn't even entertain." He leaned down, resting his palms on the covers of the bed to meet her eye to eye. "You *will* please me tonight, little thief. And once you've repaid your debt, you can leave."

She wet her lips nervously and tried not to fidget beneath his scrutiny. "Debt? I didn't even get to take anything," she protested, moving to swing her legs over the side of the bed. "Heck, I didn't even see what was in the safe." Something about the way he was towering over her was unsettling as hell and the desire to stand was overwhelming, but the whipcrack of his voice had her freezing in place.

"Did I tell you to get up, Ms. Mack?" His brows drew together in a frown so fierce she had to look away. Still, she didn't have to answer his stupid question if she didn't want to. She firmed her chin and stayed silent.

"Whether you were successful in robbing me is of no importance. Your intent was to take what was mine. Now, as penance for your transgression, you will give me what is yours."

She tamped down the anxiety and dug around for some Mary Mack spunk, managing a half laugh. "Not bloody likely."

He stood tall, looking every inch of his six-plus feet and more, and then shrugged, quirking a careless brow. "Then I will take it."

She didn't know what possessed her, but nerves got the better of her, and her mouth started running of its own accord. "I'd like to see you try."

Mon dieu, Mary, put a sock in it. The blood pounded in her ears as she waited for his response with breath held.

The corner of his mouth quirked upward, a stark contrast to the cool indifference in his eyes. "Interesting choice of words, because I've decided that you won't be seeing anything at all."

He slowly made his way around the side of the bed, every step bringing him closer, every step sending her pulse careening more wildly than the one before. When he finally stood directly before her, her whole world tilted. Her gaze flickered to his zipper and her mouth watered. She wanted him there again. Wanted to close her lips over that silky, thick head and draw him deep, one glorious inch at a time.

The yank on her ponytail was quick and sharp. A real attention-getter, and she found her head forcibly tugged back so she had no choice but to look at him.

"You're a dirty girl, Ms. Mack."

His voice was gruff, his breathing labored as he spoke. He was as affected as she was, and the power of that soared through her, lifting her higher.

"Normally I could appreciate that. But do you really think that a thief deserves the privilege of having my cock in her mouth?" His words sent a thick-as-molasses heat to settle between her hips. "You'll have to work for that."

The last thing she saw was his sinister smile, and then her world went black as he tugged something over her head.

Blindfolded.

Chapter Eight

Her palms went slick and the hair on her arms rose. The blackness was unnerving as hell and she reached a hand up instinctively to yank the scrap of cloth away, but his was there to greet it. He closed his fingers around her wrist and pulled it away.

"Leave it."

His firm command stilled her struggles momentarily, but she couldn't leave it. He could do anything to her like this. She was completely vulnerable, like a fish belly-up and ready to be gutted.

Right as she was about to let full-blown panic take hold, the fingers in her hair tightened, tugging once. Then again. Not hard enough to hurt. Just hard enough to feel. For some reason, it was enough. The contact centered her, gave her a focal point to cling to on this spinning, wild ride.

"Leave it," he said again.

She focused on the sensation of his strong fingers covering hers. The grip of his hand in her hair. The sound of the breath sawing in and out of his lungs, and she knew with utmost certainty that he was every bit as vulnerable as she was right now. Two words and she could make this whole scenario come crashing down. Two words and it would be over.

Two words she had not a single intention of uttering.

She wriggled from his grasp and let her hand fall to her side, hoping the euphoria she was feeling didn't make her voice tremble. "Fine then, Mr. Welter. You win. If you get off on bedding an unwilling woman who has no interest in you whatsoever, then go ahead." Mary Mack had apparently picked up a British accent somewhere along the way, but she went with it. "I won't stop you."

Every nerve in her body was at full attention, waiting for his next move. He released her hair and a long moment passed in silence. What the hell was he doing? She tipped her head, straining to hear any sign of movement, but there was nothing. No sound, no new smell, though her senses seemed enhanced by her lack of vision. It was as though she was entirely alone.

After a moment, she worked up the nerve to call him by name, but there was no response.

Was this her punishment for asking questions? He'd left her here? Alone? Surely not…

Another thirty seconds passed with nothing but the sound of her own erratic breathing to remind her that she wasn't deaf as well as blind. Then, out of nowhere, it all changed. The heady scent of his musky cologne filled her nostrils, the ambient heat of his body radiated against her skin, sending goose bumps up her arms.

He was close.

Close enough to touch, and she balled her fists to resist the urge to reach for him. She was his prisoner, not his date. She didn't allow herself to remember how much she'd enjoyed that as well.

A single finger traced her lips, and she instinctively

opened her mouth to take it in, to taste it, but it was gone in the next instant.

Cool air greeted her chest as he opened the trench coat, one button at a time. He slid it off slowly, exposing her to his gaze. Her heart beat triple time and she held her breath. He was looking at her, half-naked right now, and not seeing his face was killing her. Her nipples went taut and achy as a low sigh of appreciation escaped him, his minty breath washing over her face.

"Very nice, Ms. Mack."

She willed him to touch her then, squinting tight, hoping he would do that magic thing again where he seemed to read her thoughts. Her hopes were dashed as she sensed him moving away, taking his body heat and mouthwatering scent with him.

Next came the heels. He unbuckled the slim ankle strap with exquisite slowness that unearthed memories of the garter incident and she shuddered. If tonight ended even half as spectacularly as that one had, she could die happy.

"Stand," he muttered, his voice thick and gritty. The single-word command shouldn't have sent a rush of moisture to her core, but it did. She obeyed without question, using the bed to guide her and then rising to her feet.

His warm breath stirred her hair as he gripped the leather waistband that stretched across her hips. He tugged the pants down to her ankles, patting her bottom lightly, urging her to step out of them.

She stood like that for a long time. Stock-still, back straight, breasts thrust forward, hoping against hope that her body pleased him.

"I believe we have a problem, Ms. Mack."

Her heart dove to her toes and all the defenses she'd let drop snapped back into place. She crossed her arms over her chest and took a step back. His hands closed over her shoulders, halting her backward motion.

"Don't ever cover yourself from me. You're too beautiful to hide," he murmured softly before his voice regained strength and the cold edge of her nemesis, Mr. Welter. "The problem is that, to my understanding, you should be naked right now, should you not?"

She could hardly think over the relief flooding through her. He seemed to really like her body, so then what?

She was naked, besides…she sucked in a breath, realizing her mistake. She'd been in such a rush to get here on time that she'd slid on underwear out of habit without giving it a second thought. And who could blame her? Leather and vaginas weren't meant to co-hab without some sort of buffer. Surely that was a rule somewhere?

"I asked you a question, Ms. Mack."

She struggled to come up with an explanation that would suffice, but only managed a whispered, "Yes."

"I'm sure we can both agree you deserve to be punished for this."

His voice was quiet, but his deep, authoritative timbre still seemed to vibrate through her. It wasn't a question, so she didn't think she was on the hook for a response, which was a good thing. She didn't know whether she agreed or disagreed.

Her brain was 100 percent certain that, if she had a vote, she would have cast it for "no punishment." But her body wasn't so sure. Her skin felt too tight, like it was awaiting something astounding.

"Grab hold of my shoulders," he ground out. She complied, reveling in their breadth and strength under the crisp cotton of his shirt. God, she'd forgotten he was still fully clothed. The thought should have bothered her, but instead it added to the fantasy. She was entirely at his mercy.

She gripped his shoulders more tightly as he dropped lower. Kneeling?

"Back into the shoes."

Ah, he liked the shoes, then. A tidbit she would tuck away for future use, maybe. A secret thrill ran through her and she meekly did his bidding, waiting patiently as he fastened the buckles. When he was done, his fingers trailed up her calves in a slow, winding caress that had her digging her fingers into his shoulders.

They skittered up her thighs before playing at the thin straps of her panties. With a quick tug, they came apart in his hand with a snap and she gasped. At this rate, she wasn't going to have any left.

"Last. Time," he growled, rising to his feet. "When you're with me like this, I want your pussy bare and ready for the taking."

Her mouth went dry and she nodded.

"Now sit, and move back against the bedpost."

She lowered herself back to the bed and scooted until she felt the cold rails of the iron headboard.

"Give me your wrists." His voice was gruff, like he was in pain, and she wanted to pull the blindfold from her eyes… read his thoughts. But she didn't. Instead, heart pounding, she did as he requested, waiting, anticipating the cold steel of cuffs, but it never came.

He crossed her wrists, and guided them high above her head, binding them together with what could only be the tattered black lace of her offending underwear, and tied them to the metal rail. Then he was gone again. For another long moment, there was silence, even more deafening than the last time, and her head whirred with possibilities. What next? How far would he push her? Her stomach clenched with a need so sharp, it hurt. God, she wanted him. But she could do nothing about it but sit and wait.

There was a rustling sound in the far corner of the suite, then a clatter. She perked up as his footfalls grew nearer.

"Open your mouth," he demanded.

Excitement lanced through her and she parted her lips. Something frozen pressed against her mouth, smooth and hard, and his voice greeted her again. "Swipe your tongue around it. Suck it." His voice was clipped. Urgent. The need to blow him away with instruction-following skills after the whole underwear debacle made her take to the task like a fucking champ. She closed her teeth around the smooth, square-shaped object and sucked lightly. No taste. No smell.

Ice.

Cold water trickled down from her mouth, over her chin, and she shivered when droplets skittered down her neck.

Her hand twitched to wipe her chin but she was met with the taut reminder of her imprisonment. She shouldn't have worried. In the next moment, a calloused thumb was tracing the line from her jaw to her lips, collecting the errant droplets. How long would he make her wait this time? Or would that be her punishment? Maybe relief from the ever-building ache would never come.

The sound of her swallowing seemed to echo through the room and she closed her teeth over the chunk of ice and bit down, cracking it in half. His low, harsh laugh only fanned the flames of the fire building in her.

"Watch those teeth, Ms. Mack."

He pulled the ice away and just as she wondered what was next, he trailed the cube down her throat, and lower, circling her collarbones, leaving a chilly path of electricity in its wake. He brushed over the tops of her breasts, once, twice, before rolling the fast-melting cube over her taut nipples.

Beads of water rolled down the curve of her breasts as he went, circling the aching peaks until a moan broke from her lips. Her skin burned with need, her blood boiled under the surface, and even the ice couldn't dull her flames. The contrast was deadly. With every droplet of water, her need only grew more intense.

"Tell me again, little thief. What were you saying about taking a woman against her will? A woman who"—he tweaked her nipple tightly between his warm fingers and she arched into him helplessly—"had no interest in me, a man like any other, at all?"

His ministrations became relentless as he played the ice over her straining breasts until they went almost numb from the near-excruciating cold, and then massaged and plucked at them with his big, warm hands. On and on it went, until her head tossed restlessly against the pillow and she struggled against her restraints.

"Rafe, please," she whispered.

He blew out a long shuddering breath. A second later, his molten mouth was on her, his tongue laving her chilled flesh, sucking her nipples hard in a steady rhythm that made her hips flutter in counterpoint.

"Ah, fuck," she moaned, too far gone now to care. She strained harder, intent now on freeing her hands from their bindings to no avail. He could be her only respite and the pleas tumbled freely from her lips. "Please, please, I do want you."

He growled with satisfaction but his mouth continued its torture as a rattle sounded by her ear. Soon another ice cube joined the party, slipping over her rib cage, sliding over her stomach, circling her belly button. His tongue followed close behind, the polar temperature dueling with the damp heat for her attention.

"Spread your legs." The words alone might have been enough to push her over the edge, but she held on, waiting for his next command. Desperate to please him as much as he was pleasing her.

When the ice circled her clit, she screamed and bucked so hard, the bed rail squealed in protest. He did it again, brushing it lightly against her overheated flesh like he was painting her with a brush. Water mixed with her own wetness and pooled between her thighs, trickling down her slit.

"Tell me, Ms. Mack." The words sounded like they were wrenched from him with a crowbar. Rusty, guttural, and raw. "Why are you so fucking wet for a man you have no interest in?"

She writhed helplessly against him, dying to squeeze her thighs together, to add that last bit of pressure she so desperately needed to push her over the edge, but she knew better. This was her punishment, and she wasn't about to add on to her sentence. Surely he was almost done?

She leaned back, sucking in air through her nose and blowing it out through her mouth. She could do this. She'd almost managed to convince herself when he slanted his mouth over her and plunged his tongue deep. A low scream built in her chest and she tensed, ready to tumble, but he tore his mouth away one moment too soon and she nearly wept.

"I'm sorry. I-I shouldn't have said that to you. I shouldn't have worn the panties." Her overloading brain floundered wildly for more things to apologize for. Anything to make him finish it. To slip a finger inside and work her until she was over the edge, cover her swollen clit with his mouth and massage it with that skillful tongue until she went spiraling into oblivion.

It was so close, she could touch it. He thumbed her clit lightly, the touch so much but not nearly enough. What did he want to hear? What would free her from this sensual torture?

She stilled and held her breath, desperately trying to feel past the hands intent on killing her with pleasure so she could focus in on him. He was breathing at least as hard as she was. The hand that caressed her shook with need. This was as much of a torture for him as it was for her. So how to throw him over the edge?

"I need it." The words tripped from her lips in a whisper. "I need it so bad. You want it too, don't you? To push that thick cock into me?"

His responding grunt was punctuated by his finger parting her and sliding into her.

"Feel it? How hot and wet I am for you?"

His finger pressed forward, rewarding her with another shallow thrust. She bounced her hips lightly and moaned.

"Fuck it," he snarled.

Elation soared through her as the bedsprings creaked. A zipper sounded, then the rustle of clothes before he returned to the bed, rough hands gripping her ankles. His strength was a constant, like one wrong move could break her, but she couldn't muster even an ounce of regret over that fact.

He lifted her legs high into the air, folding her in half until her toes nearly touched her nose and her ass was off the mattress. Then, without so much as a warning, he thrust into her with a muttered curse, his huge cock battering its way deep into her tight channel, a brutal possession.

It should have hurt, but she was so far past ready, there was nothing but razor-sharp pleasure as her body stretched to accommodate him. He held himself still for a long moment, his cock twitching inside her, setting off tiny tremors. Then he started to move, working himself in and out at a torturous pace. The drag of his flesh against hers almost too exquisite to bear.

She was dangling by a thread, preparing for free fall.

"Do you want to come on my cock now, Ms. Mack?" His voice was so low, it could've belonged to a stranger. But it didn't. It was Rafe and her body was aware of every inch of him as he took her. Her mind whirred, searching desperately for a part that was still capable of thought.

Finally, she choked, "Yes."

"Don't," he commanded through gritted teeth.

Despair washed over her. Jesus, how could she possibly not? She bit her lip hard enough to taste blood, determined to obey him in spite of her doubts that she could. Determined to stave off the impending tsunami.

But damn did he make it hard. He worked her faster, resting her ankles on his shoulders so that his fingers could dig into her ass, grinding her hips forward to meet his controlled thrusts, pushing himself deeper with every plunge. In and out, the rhythmic slap of skin against skin filling the room.

His thumbs dug deeper into her hips and she could practically feel the bruises forming, but she didn't care. The pleasure and pain were so connected, each intensifying the other, that it hardly mattered anymore. There was only one thing on her mind, and that was Rafe.

In the next moment, the blackness was gone, and cool air rushed over her face as she blinked, quickly adjusting to the dim light. She took in everything hungrily. Her ankles draped around Rafe's neck, his big hand gripping her shoe, the way his biceps rippled with every plunge, and finally, his long, thick cock, gleaming with wetness, sliding in and out of her. His thrusts became wild, and her brief reunion with sight was gone as her vision went hazy.

Don't come, she willed herself as the waves dragged her deeper and deeper. Do not *come.*

"Come," he growled, his hips working like pistons now, fucking her so hard, her teeth clacked together. "Come for me now, love."

And she did. It came on like a locomotive, tearing through her with an intensity that rocked her. "Oh my God," she chanted over and over as the shock waves crashed over her again and again. Before her body had stopped convulsing, he followed behind, throwing his head back and letting out a groan.

His eyes were closed, his neck tense, tendons standing out in stark relief as his cock twitched and bucked inside her. The movement sent her flying again and she rode him restlessly to a second, soul-rocking climax.

It took a while before she could see again, and for the blood to stop rushing in her ears. When she managed to look up, she found him staring down at her.

"You're so gorgeous, it hurts," he said simply. He slid her ankles off his shoulders, pressing a kiss to one before settling them onto the bed. "I'm going to clean up. Give me two minutes."

She watched him go, her satisfaction so complete, so all-encompassing, she almost forgot…

"Wait, I'm still tied up! Aren't you going to let me go?"

He didn't look back, his low, sexy laugh sending her senses humming. "Of course."

She slouched back and resigned herself to waiting a couple more minutes to scratch the itch on her nose, when he stuck his head out of the bathroom.

"As soon as I'm done with you."

She gaped at him incredulously. Surely, he was done…

He strode over to the safe against the far wall, supremely confident in his nakedness. Nudging the still-cracked door with a toe, he swung it open and then reached inside, retrieving a black briefcase.

He slung it onto the small dining table and flicked the catch with his thumb. "Surely you didn't think you were going to get away that easily," he murmured softly. Her jangling nerves started to get the better of her when she glanced down to see his cock already thickening and at the ready. He reached inside the case and pulled out what looked like a slim, leather-bound wand. A dozen long, thin strips of leather sprouted from the tip like a fountain.

Was that a—

"Flogger," he said softly, padding toward the bed. "Time for your punishment, Ms. Mack."

Chapter Nine

"Toy boat."

The words were out before she could even think. Watching him prowl toward her looking lethal—sexy as hell, but lethal nonetheless—with the leather strips of the flogger slapping softly against his hand? The panic had taken over.

Rafe stopped mid-stride and nodded curtly. "Roger that."

The shadow of regret passing over his face made Courtney's stomach clench. She wasn't afraid he would truly hurt her. Not really, it was just a knee-jerk reaction to being helpless and all the possibilities that had terrified her. She opened her mouth to take it back, tell him she'd changed her mind, but he was already in motion again, setting the flogger back into the case.

He tugged on his boxers and faced her again, a warm, patient smile on his face. "I'm going to come over there and untie you now, okay?" He waited for permission before approaching her, and her stomach went flippy again.

So strange how one second, he was in total control,

dictating their every action, and now with the utterance of two silly words, he wouldn't even touch her without her explicit agreement.

While the knowledge was incredibly empowering, she was coming to the stunning realization that she liked things better before. When he'd had the reins and she had trusted him enough to manage them properly. Now she felt unsure, wishing she could fix it but not knowing how.

"You okay?" His mouth was close to her ear as his fingers worked at the knots and his warm breath sent a shiver through her.

"Yes," she said, trying to cover the quiver in her voice so he wouldn't know she was on the brink of tears. This was it. He was going to untie her, and she was going to get dressed and then they would leave separately and this would all be nothing but a memory. When the tension binding her hands together released and the scrap of cloth fell away, she'd never felt less free. This time, there was no stopping the tears.

"What's the matter?" Rafe asked, pulling the sheet up to cover her before taking her wrists gently in his hands. "Are you hurt?" The horror on his face only made her cry more.

"N-no." She hiccuped and pulled her hands away so she could use them to cover her miserable face. "I just w-wish I didn't say toy boat," she admitted.

"Is that so?"

"Yeah." She shrugged helplessly. "I don't even know why I said it. Nerves, I guess. The fear of the unknown. I hate that because I like to think I'm tougher than that."

"I think you're pretty tough, but I do agree that it's scary to try something you've never tried before, especially when you also feel helpless," he said softly. "But do you think maybe another part of the reason was that you wanted to make sure it would work?" He motioned for her to move over and then sat down on the bed next to her.

She swiped the tears away and considered his words. Was that it? Had she subconsciously needed to test the system? To test him so she could be sure he was worthy of her trust?

If so, that was crappy of her, especially since he hadn't done anything to make her distrust him so far. "I'm sorry. As you know, I had some…issues in the past with a guy." She stopped short and let out a slow breath, debating how much she wanted to share.

Rafe laid a gentle hand on her hip and squeezed. "You don't have to talk about it if you don't want to."

Oddly enough, after a few seconds of soul searching, she realized that wasn't the case at all. "I want to. It's just hard because it's embarrassing. I was so dumb and naive."

"I'm not going to judge you, Courtney. We all make mistakes."

"His name was Wes," she began slowly. "He was an assistant professor in the anatomy department of the grad school I went to. I crushed on him almost immediately, but he had a girlfriend and I was too busy with school to get seriously involved with a guy in any case. We met again at an alumni dinner a year after I graduated, and we clicked."

The memory was a weird one, because she could still see the Wes she thought she knew through those rose-colored glasses, but hot on its heels was the image of real Wes. Controlling Wes. Sternly disapproving Wes.

She wriggled until she was seated, using the headboard as a back support, before she continued. "Anyway, I won't bore you with the details but he was everything I could have wanted. Everything I'd ever dreamed of in a guy, until we moved in together. It was like night and day—"

"Dr. Jekyll and Mr. Hyde," he finished softly.

"Right. He started picking my friends and, after a while, I had none left. As archaic as it sounds, I had a curfew." She blew a lock of hair from her face and shook her head, trying her damnedest to fight the waves of humiliation rolling over her. "A grown woman. With a curfew. It was never spoken out loud, so it didn't seem so bad, but we both knew if I wasn't home by nine p.m. there would be hell to pay."

"Did he hit you?"

The cold, contained fury in Rafe's voice almost made her feel sorry for the criminals he dealt with on a day-to-day basis. He could be terrifying. But not with her.

"No," she assured him. The tension that had gripped his body relented some as he settled in closer to her, his hip a comforting weight against her bent knee. "I think that's the part that makes me feel the stupidest. Maybe if he hit me, I'd have a better excuse for staying so long."

"Sometimes emotional scars are worse than physical ones. I think you should focus on the strength it took to walk away. That's not easy to do when you have a history with someone, and you've invested your life and time into a person. A lot of people never leave."

She digested that and held it close, letting his kind words wrap around her like a blanket. "If things hadn't escalated, who knows how long I would've stayed? But he crossed the line. I'd been working at a hospital for about a year and there was a doctor there who I became friendly with. He was a great guy, married with two sweet kids. He sent me a totally innocuous joke e-mail one day and Wes had taken to checking my accounts. He actually came into the hospital and created a huge scene, ranting at the guy in front of staff and patients."

Her hands shook at the memory, but Rafe's steady grip on her hip calmed her enough that she was able to continue.

"It was quite literally the last straw. I packed my stuff and was gone the next day but it obliterated my career at the hospital. Rumors started. It caused a rift between my doctor friend and his wife that I later found out took months to repair. Eventually, I had to quit. I decided I needed a fresh start, and you know the rest."

He nodded and worked up a little smile. "You moved to Rhode Island and took our tiny state by storm."

"I don't know about that," she said with a laugh. Maybe talking about her past hadn't absolved her of her part in what had taken place, but she felt a hundred pounds lighter having shared it with Rafe.

"Well, for what it's worth, I'm proud of you for getting out."

"Thanks."

The silence that followed was the most uncomfortable she'd ever experienced, but she couldn't bring herself to break it. The elephant was still very much in the room and she didn't know how to approach it. Rafe shifted, moving to stand, and her heart took a nosedive.

"Don't go."

She might not know exactly how this was all going to turn out, but the thought of letting him walk away was more than she could bear.

"I want a mulligan."

• • •

Rafe pushed himself to his feet, trying to get a handle on his clamoring pulse and the raging need to climb back into bed with Courtney and forget those two words.

Toy boat.

So telling that she'd chosen them. Toy. Something to play with. A fun distraction. Boat. A getaway. A vehicle to transport a person out into the unknown. Toy boat. Her get-out-of-subbing-free card, and she'd played it. Now, as a dom, it was his job to accept it with grace and end the scene, which he had.

Only, fuck, now she wanted a mulligan. Would he be taking advantage if he allowed it? Technically, the scene had ended and beginning again would be a new experience for them both. Technically.

He blew out a sigh and stared down at her, regret bitter on his tongue. She looked so hopeful, so vulnerable, he hated the thought of crushing that. He'd been encouraging her to be open to him, and now that she'd taken his words to heart, he was about to throw them back at her.

Anyone who thought it was easy being on top was dead wrong. There was a lot of responsibility, and he was determined not to fuck it up.

"Please, Rafe. I...want this. I want you. And I want to try."

Her wide eyes drifted over to the case that sat on the table across the room and his gut tightened. He fought the urge to relent instantly. To forget everything else and pick up right where they'd left off.

"I know you regret using your out, but I need to know that you won't be afraid to use it again if this is too much for you. I was a little bummed for a second this time, but only because I was looking forward to being with you longer. Safe-ing out doesn't mean that I will think less of you or be disappointed in you. All it means is that today, right now, you aren't ready for whatever it was we were doing. Do you understand what I'm saying?"

It was important that she did. It was everything.

She nodded but he pushed harder, needing the words.

"I need you to trust me enough to tell me the truth. I need to trust you enough to know that you will. And you need to be sure right now."

The fact that it took her almost a full minute should've made him nervous, but it had the exact opposite effect. It gave him the most profound sense of appreciation for Courtney and her nature. Her face was a mask of contemplation and when she finally nodded—one time—and spoke, her voice rang with total conviction.

"I'm sure."

He closed his eyes for a long moment, trying to stay calm even as every nerve in his body went on high alert. More time with Courtney and it wouldn't cost him a scene. He was jazzed as fuck about it, but shut those thoughts down fast. He was a guy fresh off a smoking-hot sexual encounter. It was natural to feel closer to her than he had before, at least temporarily. It had nothing to do with their impromptu date or their heart-to-heart and everything to do with chemistry. Once the dopamine had faded, and he was home in his own bed, everything would go back to the way it was before.

She leaned forward then and kissed his jaw, letting the sheet fall away until her breast nudged his biceps, and his thoughts disintegrated into dust.

"I'm ready to accept my punishment, Mr. Welter," she murmured.

His cock stiffened at her words and he fought every instinct, demanding that he press her back against the bed, spread her legs wide, and fuck her senseless. It would be so good.

But not as good as it would be if he stuck to the scene. He could take them both to the edge of sanity if he maintained his cool here.

He stood and made his way across the room in purposeful strides. "Present to me on all fours, Ms. Mack." He took the flogger from the case and turned to face her again. She stared at him, wide-eyed.

"Like"—she rolled onto her stomach and lifted herself onto her palms and knees, sending him a questioning glace over her shoulder—"this?"

He swallowed hard at the sight of her bare ass, plump,

round, and ready. "No." He kept his voice low. Deliberate, in spite of the riot going on inside him. "Lean forward onto your elbows, forehead against the mattress."

She dropped the top half of her body low as he'd asked and just when he thought the picture couldn't get prettier, it did. Her bowed back was elegant, the dip of her spine a dream. His hands ached to touch her, but he stayed where he was, sucking in long, steadying breaths.

"I want you to close your eyes now."

"Okay, they're closed."

Her voice was trembling and he resisted the urge to make sure it was from excitement and not fear. He'd know soon enough, and like he'd told her. As much as she had to trust him to respect her boundaries, he had to trust her to utter her safe word if she needed to.

He crossed the room, committing the stunning sight to memory before rounding to the side of the bed, lining up next to her knees.

"Do you know what happens to thieves, Ms. Mack?" he asked softly.

She shook her head against the mattress but didn't respond verbally. Apparently Ms. Mack wasn't quite as ballsy as she'd been earlier.

"Normally they go to prison, don't they? So this is pretty nice of me, wouldn't you say?"

She nodded and made a little squeaking sound he took as a yes.

"In light of my kindness, after each lash, I'd like you to thank me. Is that understood?" A long pause this time, and he knew she was fighting her own ornery nature that demanded she argue. He almost cracked a smile, imagining the names she was probably calling him in her head, but then she nodded and suddenly shit wasn't funny anymore.

He kept his tone clipped. "I need the words, Ms. Mack.

Are we clear?"

"Yes," she whispered.

The buzzing in his ears increased tenfold and he looked down to see that his hands were shaking with need.

Well, fuck.

. . .

It was so quiet, she wondered if he'd even heard her. Not willing to give him any excuse to call it off after her safe-word slipup, she swallowed hard and repeated herself, more loudly this time.

"Y-yes." God, her legs were trembling, her pulse was pounding, and she was so wet, she was almost embarrassed by it.

Almost.

"Excellent. And when we're done, if you're very good, I'll let you ride my cock."

His bold words and the raw heat of his tone sent a thrill skittering through her before settling between her hips. She wondered briefly if anyone had ever died from need.

He moved in closer and laid a warm hand on her lower back. "Ready?"

She nodded, stiffening, bracing herself for the first blow, but it never came.

"I need you to take a deep breath and relax. Let your muscles go loose. Try to embrace the pain rather than fight it, all right?"

She willed her body to go lax, diverting her attention toward scrunching up her face instead. The clock in the room was digital, but she swore she could hear the seconds tick by interminably as she waited for the sting of the flogger.

Instead, the strong, gentle hand on her back dipped lower to stroke the curve of her ass, kneading and rubbing.

Fingertips drifted close to the crevice there and then lower to where all the heat and moisture in her body had seemed to pool. She gasped and pushed back against him, urging those fingers to dip lower, to slide—

Smack!

Courtney stiffened, the pain of the leather straps streaking over her ass cheek. Before she could pull away, that hand was in motion again, massaging the offending spot. It still stung, heck, his firm touch even intensified it, but the sensation went from white-hot pain to molten pleasure.

She pulsed back against him, again urging him to use his fingers to take her over the edge. God knew it wouldn't take much. Right when she found herself wondering if anyone had ever come from having their ass rubbed, suddenly, he pulled his hand away.

"Where's my thank you, Ms. Mack?"

His voice was low and steady, but thick with need, and she reveled in the fact that he was as affected as she was. It made it so much easier to let the last of her inhibitions go. To hand him the keys and let him drive them both to the edge of sanity.

"Thank you, Mr. Welter."

Now please, again, she wanted to beg, but knew it would get her nowhere. She stayed perfectly still and waited, and soon her patience was rewarded.

The second blow was harder than the first but not in the same spot. She almost cried out but held back, biting her lip, waiting for the hot sting to magically morph into something else. Sure enough, even as her ass throbbed, a rush of heat pooled between her slightly spread legs.

"I can see how wet you are from here." This time, there was nothing calm about him. His voice was all grit and lust. She couldn't resist the urge to shake her bottom, lean deeper into her stance to lure him in, draw him closer, will him to touch her there.

"But you didn't thank me again, Ms. Mack," he growled.

This time, no touching before the next blow, and it was a doozy. She couldn't hold back her cry as the leather came down on her sensitive flesh.

"Thank you," she murmured, when the discomfort subsided enough that she could catch her breath.

"Good."

She went warm with his praise.

Smack.

She tried to separate the ache from the ecstasy as the blows rained, sometimes in slow succession as he massaged her in between, sometimes two in a row. Flames licked her from head to toe and she pressed her upper body against the mattress, her hard nipples aching for contact.

"Move toward the foot of the bed."

She didn't hesitate, skittering a few feet down until her toes touched the edge of the mattress. He rounded the bed, moving to stand directly behind her.

Smack.

She tried not to move as, upon her murmured thanks, the flogger dropped to the floor and he squeezed her stinging cheeks hard in both hands.

"Mmpmh," she groaned, wanting to pull away and push closer at the same time.

"You're amazing. Ass so beautiful, with my marks on you, pink and hot, your pussy swollen and wet and waiting for me." He squeezed again, kneading her heated flesh, sending another bolt of pleasure/pain coursing through her. "You took your punishment so well," he said, climbing onto the bed next to her and leading her wrist toward him. "Take my cock out."

She was shaking so badly she wondered if she could manage the job, but when she saw the broad head of him thrusting out the top of his underwear, she was so desperate to have him inside her, nothing could have stopped her.

She jerked the boxers down, not even bothering to take them all the way off, and threw a knee over his hips to straddle him. Settling lower, she took his thick length in her hand and squeezed, loving the hiss it elicited from him.

"Fuck me," he demanded.

She tore her gaze away from his cock and met his gaze. His eyes were like glittering chunks of onyx, his jaw so tense, he looked to be in pain. She slid down, intent on taking it slow, but he would have none of it. The second their bodies touched, he gripped her hips and flexed, pressing his hard length deep.

She couldn't breathe, couldn't think. She tried to pull away. It was too intense, too much, but he was there, murmuring soft words of encouragement as he palmed her ass and pressed firmly again, sliding her farther onto his rigid cock.

"That's my girl. There it is. Take it."

She shook from the effort of remaining still, desperate for the release that was just around the corner but not wanting this delicious torture to end.

"They aren't numbered, you know," he murmured, as if reading her mind. He swirled his hips and ground against her, anchoring her against him with both hands on her ass. The sweet tingle and throb came back with a vengeance and the combination of that along with him buried deep was too much.

She rose and slammed back down, almost to the point of pain, and her body stretched to accommodate him. Each nerve ending lit up and she exploded over his hard cock. She couldn't move, she was so caught up in the haze of pleasure crashing over her, but he was there, cupping her hips, using them to work her over him again and again, taking the flames higher and higher.

"Jesus, oh my God!"

Her scream mingled with his shout as he convulsed beneath her, pinning her to him. His face was a mask of ecstasy as his cock jerked wildly inside her even as her own orgasm seemed to stretch on and on.

They stayed like that for a long minute, until their breathing slowed and their hearts stopped clamoring. She'd just come to the realization that she was going to have to climb off him and step away from the haven of his body, when he hauled her forward to sprawl on top of him, and laughed softly into her hair.

"Well done, Ms. Mack."

His tone was playful, but tinged with something else. Satisfaction. Dare she hope, happiness? A warm sense of pride warmed her from the inside out as he slid a hand up her back to cover her nape before toying with her hair.

If she made him feel even half as good as he made her feel, then she'd done something right. She was going to enjoy every second of this. Seize the moment. Soak it all in. She refused to think about what tomorrow would bring. Refused to consider what things would be like after their last scene.

And she wasn't even going to contemplate how in the world she was ever going to go back to real life after the fantasy that was Rafe Davenport.

Chapter Ten

"Where do you think you're going?"

She'd been rehashing the night with Rafe over in her head for the thousandth time when she heard it. The whining, nasally voice sent a wave of disgust through her, and she paused on her way to the elevator, fixing a tight smile to her lips.

"I'm going home, Barry. Like people do when their shifts are over."

Her two fellow nurses, Rhonda and Shelby, suddenly got really busy—looking uncomfortable, chattering softly to each other, and pushing papers around at the main desk a few feet away.

Barry glared, his watery gaze locked on hers. Courtney shifted the stack of patient files to her other arm. She'd planned to take them down to Records on her way out, but a sinking dread settled over her at the cold gleam in her supervisor's gaze.

She'd seen it before. Several times, actually, since he'd started that spring. He actively enjoyed ruining people's days.

He took joy in the misery of others. He treated employees who were under his pay grade like they were garbage. In a word, he was a big, fat asshole, with a capital A, and he got off on abusing his relative power.

"Chyeah, about that. Look, I wish I could spare you, but it looks like we're going to need you to stick around for a double shift again tonight." The faux regret pinched his thin lips, but didn't make it to his beady ice-blue eyes.

Exhaustion settled over her like a water-saturated blanket. Weeks of screwy sleep schedules due to last-minute extra shifts were taking a serious toll on her, and the thought of spending another eight hours at work was enough to make her throat ache with frustration.

"Look, Barry, I haven't been getting a lot of sleep and I—"

His thick brows came together in a thunderous frown even as his weak chin wobbled with indignation. "If your evening activities are too rigorous for you to be in tip-top shape to do your job, then maybe you need to prioritize better, Ms. DeLollis. Now either you can take those files down and come back on up or you can run the risk of me finding another nurse who is a little more dedicated than you are to fill your position."

Rhonda and Shelby had done away with the pretense and had gone silent as they watched the scene before them, sympathy written all over their faces. Barry had delivered a pretty low blow, but maybe he was partly right.

Granted, she hadn't been scheduled to work the day after her night at the hotel with Rafe, but even now two days later, she was a little tired. Guilt nipped her hard and she was about to apologize when something stopped her.

Who the hell did this guy think he was, treating her that way? He might be her supervisor, but that didn't give him the right to talk to her like she was a piece of crap on his shoe.

She straightened and returned Barry's glare with a vengeance. "What I do with my time off is none of your concern, and the insinuation that I would ever come to work in a condition that could be detrimental to my patients infuriates me."

She strode to the long metal desk and set the folders she'd been holding onto it with a snap before whipping around to face him again.

"My contract is for five shifts a week. When there is an emergency and they need extra hands on deck, I'm never anything but accommodating. But if you think you're going to treat me the way you do and then try to shame me into taking a back-to-back shift so I can do a bunch of busywork that could be done any time, then you're sadly mistaken."

His eyes practically rolled to the back of his head as he advanced closer. Close enough that she put a hand up in warning. He stopped short, but the rage pouring off him was palpable. "I'll be talking to Leslie about this."

Courtney admired and respected their head nurse, and hated the idea of their relationship being tainted by this man, but she ignored the tiny voice in her head that told her to apologize and instead met Barry head-on.

"You certainly will, because I'm going to file a complaint against you, which I should've done months ago. Part of your job, besides respecting people's boundaries and personal space"—she sent a pointed glance at the few inches between them—"and keeping morale up, is making sure hospital funds are being used wisely. Imagine what the bosses would say if they realized that half the time you make us stay late and work overtime it's purely for your own sadistic enjoyment and not because we actually need to be here?"

One of the nurses behind her whispered "Damn straight" under her breath, but Courtney was focused on Barry, who had gone from furious to sweating and nervous in a matter of seconds. He wet his lips and stepped back. "Look, I did need some help with a project for tonight, but no big deal. We'll just let this go and—"

"We won't let it go, because if it's not me, it will be someone else and no one should have to put up with this." She stepped away now, feeling better by the second. Finally standing up to him felt amazing, and she was almost giddy with the sense of freedom. "Make sure those files get to Records before midnight. My shift is officially over."

She made her best effort not to flounce, keeping her head high but her steps slow and measured. No point in making it more of scene than it needed to be. So obviously, that meant leaping up and clicking her heels together like the leprechaun from the Lucky Charms commercial was probably out, but damn, did she feel like it.

Once the elevator doors closed behind her, though, she did a quick, impromptu jig. She'd effectively shut down Brutal Barry and, once she filed her complaint, hopefully it would be forever.

By the time she got home, the euphoria had begun to fade, but not the newfound confidence. She'd finally done it. Stood up for herself with her boss and the world hadn't ended or anything. In fact, she'd never felt better.

She made her way into the kitchen and tossed her purse and keys onto the table. Leafing through her mail, she strolled into the living room and stopped in her tracks. Something felt off. A chill ran through her and she glanced around the room, gaze darting left and right. Seemed all right; everything was in its place.

She felt it before she saw it. A breeze tickling her nape. She spun around to see the dining room curtain fluttering gently against the windowsill. She never left the house with the windows open. Never ever.

"Rafe?" she called, praying she'd hear his silky baritone

in response, while simultaneously plotting his death for scaring the shit out of her. But there was no answer to her call.

"Hello?" She walked slowly toward the window, envelopes falling from her icy hands to the hardwood floor when she saw the shards of glass and half a shoe print. Jamming a hand into the pocket of her scrubs, she drew out her cell phone and dialed. *Please answer, please answer.*

"Davenport," a low voice barked.

"Rafe? It's Courtney. Were you…here earlier, by any chance?" She already knew the answer, he had a key, of course he hadn't come in through the window, but the question came on autopilot.

"Was I where?" he asked, his tone going from all-business detective mode to perplexed. Like he had no clue what she was talking about, as she'd expected.

Not good.

"M-my house?" she whispered, moving quickly and quietly on shaking legs to the kitchen door.

"No. What's going on? Why are you whispering?" Concern colored his tone and he'd gone back to detective-mode barking.

She strained to hear any sounds from upstairs as she skulked toward the butcher's block and slid a knife from its sheath. "My dining room window is broken and there is a muddy shoe print on the floor. Someone was in my house."

"Listen to me carefully, Courtney. Go to the nearest exit and get to a neighbor's house, immediately."

She nodded, forgetting he couldn't see her, and continued her path past the pantry and to the back door. Juggling the phone in one hand and the knife in the other, she inched the door open as quietly as possible and stepped through.

"Damn it, are you there?"

"Yes," she hissed. "Yes, I just got out of the house and am

going to Anita and Drew's across the street."

"I'm getting in my car now. I'll be there in eight minutes or less."

She didn't bother closing up behind her, the need to sprint too strong to resist. "Okay. I'm already crossing the street, and there's no one coming after me, so that's good," she panted, panic making good breath control impossible.

"Stay on the phone with me until you get there and confirm someone is home."

She could hear his siren over the receiver and just that and the knowledge he was coming calmed her some. Churning legs ate up the short distance and she arrived on Anita's doorstep less than a minute later. She knocked frantically, still checking behind her obsessively. It seemed unlikely that a burglar would run her down, but at that point, nothing seemed impossible.

"Hey, neighbor, wha—" Anita's smiling face crumpled as she took in the sight before her. Brown gaze locked on to the knife in Courtney's hand and she took a faltering step back. "Jesus, what's going on?"

"Someone broke into my house," Courtney blurted, handing the knife over, hilt first. "The police are coming and I need somewhere to wait."

"Of course, of course, come in." Anita tugged her into the foyer and called up the stairs to her husband. "Drew, come down here."

"You're good?" Rafe's clipped voice sounded over the line and Courtney nodded inanely.

"Yes. They're here. It's the blue house on the corner."

He disconnected without another word and Courtney slipped her phone back into her pocket. Her concerned neighbors huddled around her, offering tea and kind words, but she couldn't stop shaking. She wouldn't feel better until Rafe came. Once he got there, everything would be all right.

And that realization? Was scarier than a robber any day.

...

"Thank you so much again, Mr. and Mrs. Brenton. You've been very helpful," Rafe said and then closed the door behind him. Courtney was tucked under his arm and although he knew she was all right to walk on her own two feet, he couldn't bring himself to let her go yet.

"You okay?" he asked for what had to be the tenth time in as many minutes. She was probably sick of hearing it, but until the icy fear wedged in his chest started to thaw some, he was going to keep asking.

To her credit, she answered him like it was the first time. "Yeah, I'm good. Just shook up some. I'll be fine."

He nodded grimly, looking both ways as he led her across the street back toward her house. She'd be fine all right, but him? That was another story. He'd done a sweep of her house and found it empty, but someone had definitely been there. The jewelry box on her dresser had been cleaned out and her mattress had been overturned. The burglar had ignored bigger stuff like the flat-screen TV in favor of trying for easy-to-carry items and cash. Luckily, Courtney wasn't the money-under-the-mattress type, but she was out a set of diamond earrings her parents had given her, a set of gold bangle bracelets, and a brand-new laptop.

When he thought of how much worse it could have been, his guts cramped.

"I can't breathe," she mumbled, and he realized he was holding her so tight, her face was smashed against his underarm.

"Sorry."

"It's okay. Thanks for getting here so fast. I probably should've called 911 but…"

He didn't care about the why, he was glad she hadn't. He'd been able to assemble the crew he wanted to come check for fingerprints and see if they could get anything on the shoe print. The techs had left once they got what they needed, but it wasn't looking good. He still had to talk to two more of the neighbors, but so far, no prints other than the shoe and no one had seen or heard anything. There had been a rash of robberies a few blocks away and he had a bad feeling this was the same guy, but they had little to go on, and since they were committed when no one was home, these types of cases often dropped to the bottom of the pile.

That was good and bad. Good, because this burglar didn't want violence—he wanted to get in, get what he needed, and get out. Bad, because it might never get solved and that meant that a man had broken into Courtney's home, invaded her privacy, scared the shit of out of her, and made her feel insecure. And that? That made him want to kill the motherfucker.

"You're doing it again." Her voice was muffled and he released her, taking her elbow instead.

"I'm not going to faint or anything, you know. I'm sorry I scared you. I know I overreacted but—"

"You reacted exactly the way you should have." He didn't release her arm, using it to lead her up her front stairs as he fished around for the key she'd left him. "You called the police, me, and you vacated the premises. Textbook. I'm really proud of you."

She cleared her throat. "Um, thanks. You know, the back door's not locked. I left it open when I ran out."

"I locked it," he said simply. Dusk had fallen and the house was nearly dark when he swung the door open. Courtney froze in the entranceway.

"C-can you turn the light on?" she whispered.

He flicked on the switch behind him and she let out a long

sigh of relief. Maybe it was a good thing they hadn't gotten any prints. If he'd been able to ID the perp, he didn't know if he could've stopped himself from making sure the bastard wound up as afraid of the dark as Courtney was right now.

Her gaze flickered immediately to the window and she closed her eyes for a second, taking a steadying breath. "Thanks for getting rid of the glass and boarding it up. I don't think I could've slept."

"Not a problem. Why don't you have a seat? I can make you some tea or something."

"I'd rather have a beer, I think," she admitted with a wan smile. Her cheeks were still chalk white, and something to take the edge off didn't seem like a bad idea.

"Sure, I'll get it. Go sit."

She seemed like she wanted to argue, but did as he asked, padding across the oak floor to the large sectional couch that took up the center of the living room.

He headed into the kitchen and pawed around until he found a couple beers, a bottle opener, and one glass. When he returned to the living room, he found Courtney huddled into the couch cushions with a tattered pink blanket over her.

"You cold?" He eyed her hard, wondering if he'd missed signs of shock, and if she wasn't as fine as she claimed to be, but she shook her head and faced him with a clear gaze.

"No. This is the blanket I had when I was a kid. Makes me feel...comfy."

And safe, he added mentally.

He sat down next to her, opened her beer, and poured it into the glass.

She murmured her thanks and accepted the drink before twisting to face him head-on. "It doesn't seem fair, does it? That someone thinks they have the right to come into your home and take things that don't belong to them?"

"It's not fair," he agreed and then popped the cap off his

own beer and took a swig. He must have looked as grim and angry as he felt, because she laid a hand on his arm.

"I'm sorry to keep harping on it. This was nothing in the scheme of things. No one got hurt, no one…anyway, I know you've seen and dealt with so much worse…"

He could hear the pity in her voice as she struggled with the words to say. Which meant she knew about Monica. He'd figured it would come up eventually and either Cat would tell her or Galen would mention it. He racked his brain for some pithy brush-off, but shocked himself.

"It was the worst day of my life."

She squeezed his biceps reassuringly, and the words started to flow, out of control.

"I told her we should go out. She had a big test to study for and I didn't want her to spend the whole afternoon cooking, but she wouldn't have it. She was set on making me crab legs." He drained half the beer bottle and set it down. "I don't even like fucking crab legs."

He scrubbed a hand over his eyes and tried to picture her face. She'd been the exact opposite of Courtney. Black hair, dark eyes, leaner, not so curvy. The details were fuzzy now. He knew there'd been a dimple. Just one, but he couldn't remember on which side anymore. And freckles, but it was a strain to recall the pattern of them. He didn't think of her every day anymore, which was part blessing and part curse, because on days he remembered, the guilt over days he'd forgotten was almost crippling.

"It changed my life," he admitted. "From my career path to the way I thought about the world. Looking back, I can't say that those changes were for the better. I am what I am now, but you don't have to let this one event change you." She started to protest and he held up a hand. "I know it's not the same thing, but it was a violation. You can either choose to believe that this was one bad person at one bad time, give yourself a day or two to be pissed off, sad, and scared, and move on, or you can let it color your view of the world entirely, and fester."

She toyed with the ragged edges of her blanket as she contemplated his words. "Like I did with Wes," she murmured. Not angrily, which was good. "That's exactly what I did. I let him shake my confidence and keep me from trying to find another, healthier relationship. It's been like he's still controlling me and we're not even together anymore."

She settled more deeply into the cushion, suddenly looking exhausted. He patted her legs, urging her to put them on his lap. "That's enough talk for now. You've had a hell of an evening. Why don't you rest for a few minutes? I'll hang here and finish my beer, watch some TV until you want to go to bed."

She hesitated and then nodded, setting her beer on the coffee table. "I appreciate it. I'm just not ready to be alone yet." He covered her calf with his hand and rubbed in slow, soothing circles. Her eyes drifted closed and a few minutes later, she was snoring softly.

Instead of watching TV, he watched her sleep for a while, and thought of ways he could help her feel more secure. Maybe he'd suggest she get a dog. Odds were almost zero that the burglar would come back and she lived in a relatively low-crime area, but a dog would give her a sense of security as well as provide some much-needed comfort for those inevitable nights that she felt alone and scared.

Or you could help her with that.

No, he couldn't. They had two scenes left together, and tonight had served as a terrible reminder of exactly why he'd avoided getting close to another woman since Monica. He closed his eyes and relived the moments on the phone with Courtney, when she'd told him someone had broken in. He could almost picture her there, with the knife they'd left at the Brentons', tiptoeing toward the door. Jesus Christ, what if someone had still been in the house? What if that person had used that knife against her?

He sucked down the rest of the beer to wash the bitter taste of fear from his mouth before looking down at her again. Her face was so peaceful and trusting in sleep, his heart gave a squeeze.

Yeah, two more scenes, then it was time to walk away. Too bad it felt like he'd be leaving a little piece of himself behind.

Chapter Eleven

She was so warm, so cozy, she didn't want to move. But, damn, her back was getting stiff. She tried to roll to her belly, but the wall stopped her.

When the wall then inhaled and let out a slow breath, she froze.

Not a wall.

Rafe.

His arm tightened around her, and he grunted as her bottom lined up more fully with his hips.

She stared into the darkness, at a loss. Last she remembered, she'd drifted off on the couch with her feet on him. At some point, he must have fallen asleep as well, and somehow they'd wound up tangled together on the big sectional. Not that she was complaining. He felt amazing. Odd how she'd just gotten robbed, but with Rafe's body spooned around hers, she'd never felt so safe.

"You awake?" he murmured, his voice husky with sleep.

She wanted to lie. To lie there in the comfort of his sure embrace for a little longer before he pulled away. Instead, she nodded. "Yeah." She swallowed hard and waited, but he didn't move.

"You doing okay?"

She was doing fine, except that slow, sexy burn in her belly was starting to spread, the same as it did whenever he touched her. "Mm-hmm."

"Good. You scared the shit out of me, you know."

The admission shouldn't have made her happy, but it so did. Pulse banging, she gave an experimental wriggle that brought their bottom halves in, snug. The long, thick evidence of his arousal branded her ass through the thin cotton of her scrubs and sent a thrill through her.

"Courtney," he groaned, a warning in his voice.

"Rafe?" she responded boldly, not bothering to hide the challenge there. It was terrifying and exhilarating all at once. She was taking a huge chance here. This wasn't part of the deal, but there was nothing wrong with a little renegotiation.

After last night, it had become abundantly clear to her that when the chips were down, there was one person she'd wanted to call. Whether he was willing to admit it or not, this thing between them had already gone far deeper than just sex. It was time for her to start fighting for what she wanted.

He didn't seem to need much coaxing at the moment, though. His hand trailed up from her hip, dragging her shirt with it. At some point in the night, she must have stripped off her bra and tossed it because when his warm palm covered her breast, it was flesh on flesh, and she gasped. Goose bumps broke out on her arms as his fingertips teased her while his teeth nipped her earlobe.

"That's so nice," she whispered, loving the delicious pull of need that accompanied his touch. The pace was slow, leisurely, like a long summer stroll in the sunshine. She rocked back against him and sighed. By the time he rolled her onto her back and slid her pants and underwear off, she was a mass of achy need. He stood, stripping off his own clothes, before lowering himself on top of her, wedging his muscular thigh between hers.

"Your skin is so soft," he murmured as he slipped his hand over her stomach and lower. "And here. So wet. So welcoming." He dipped between her folds to rub her center in slow, steady circles.

"So hot," he groaned in a pained voice. "You make me crazy," he murmured, his voice so full of longing, it was all the encouragement she needed.

She strained forward, biting her lip as the tension wound tighter and tighter.

His low whispers spurred her on, a climax glimmering on the horizon. She fluttered her hips helplessly, her motions almost frantic. So close… He flexed a finger deep inside her, sending her hurling off the precipice.

She came hard, shudders racking her body. Dimly, even as her muscles contracted and flexed, she realized he was leaving her, moving that delicious pressure. She wanted to cry out, to tell him she wasn't done yet, but an instant later, words were impossible as he covered her body with his and slid his cock deep in one long thrust.

Aftershocks still tore through her and her inner walls clenched over him. The sensation was so sublime she could barely keep a thought in her head.

"That's what I wanted to feel," he said, his breathing so labored, it came out on a gasp. "Let me feel it again, love."

His hand snaked between them, massaging the sensitive bundle of nerves again even as he worked his cock deeper, nudging against that spot deep inside her that made her shudder.

He played her like an instrument, and this time, they came together. It was slow and sweet, his name a murmured, breathy chant on her lips. She barely managed to bite back the one that kept reverberating in her head with every beat of her heart.

Don't go.

Chapter Twelve

Rafe felt the weight on his arm before he opened his eyes, but the weight on his chest was far heavier. Waking up to the tickle of long, soft hair on his cheek and the scent of shampoo in his nose triggered memories from a past life. Memories that fucking hurt. Courtney mumbled in her sleep and tucked her bottom more firmly against his hips. He didn't resist the sudden urge to caress her cheek.

He hadn't meant to stay. At least, not unless she took the bed and he took the couch. Talk about confusing things. But for some reason, after last night, he couldn't bring himself to leave when he should have. Once she calmed some, before they'd slept together, he should have promised to be on call if she needed him, contacted Cat to come by, and then left. But even after she'd snuggled in and her breathing had gotten low and slow, he kept promising himself he would, after one more minute.

Now here he was, breaking his own rules by waking up next to the first woman he'd actually slept with in over five years. He still had nothing to offer her. No promises. No future. No happily ever after.

He tugged his arm gently out from under Courtney's head and slipped off the couch as carefully as possible. He shouldn't have worried, because she didn't budge. Fist curled up against her chin, half-smile on her face, she looked like she was dreaming of puppies. That was good. She felt safe, even if it was only in sleep for now.

He found a pen and paper in the kitchen and jotted a quick note.

Had to go. If you need anything, give me a call.

—R

A hot minute later, he was out the door. He didn't have to be at work for another two hours, but he could get a jumpstart on Courtney's case if he went in early. He'd like nothing better than to be able to call and tell her that they'd found the burglar.

And because you're a chickenshit.

Stupid fucking voice didn't know when to quit.

He swung by his house to change clothes and brush his teeth before heading over to the station. By the time he got there, his head was pounding. Tension headache from too much thinking, probably. He'd been trying his damnedest to focus on the day ahead, of possible calls he could make to various CI's and try to get some tips on who might be behind the robbery, but his mind kept circling back to Courtney. The look on her face last night when they'd made...sex.

"Fuckin' A," he growled, as he strode to his desk.

"Good morning to you too, asshole." Cherry Travers, one of the detectives in his department who worked the night shift, gave him a finger wiggle from her desk, which was situated next to his. "Bad night?

"Not the best I've had." Although that was only half-true.

Part of it had been pretty fantastic. He bit back another curse.

"Why are you here so early?" The pretty brunette took a long pull from her cup of bad station coffee and he eyed it longingly.

"I have a couple things I want to look into. Friend of mine was robbed last night. I was off duty so it's not my case, but I thought I'd do some legwork to help out. You make a whole pot or…" He nodded toward her cup, interested in the answer as much as he was interested in cutting the convo short.

"Yup. But so you know, I think it's even worse than usual. When was the last time someone washed that pot?"

He shrugged and crossed the utilitarian room to the break room. "You're supposed to wash those?"

She laughed and dropped her head back down to finish the paperwork she'd been working on.

The rest of his day flew by in such a haze, between calls that got him nowhere and his regular work, that he didn't realize he hadn't even stopped for lunch. He checked his phone again to see if Courtney had called, but she hadn't. There was a short group text from Cat letting him, Galen, Lacey, and Courtney know that she and Shane were grilling if anyone wanted to stop by for a burger on their way home. Courtney had already responded with a yes.

He mulled it over, wondering if it wouldn't be better for them to get some distance after last night, but then his stomach growled. Might as well kill two birds with one stone. He wanted to see her face, make sure she was okay, check to see if she'd called to have the window replaced and all that, plus he was starving.

"Davenport." His lieu stood over his desk casting a shadow that was as wide as it was long. Mrs. Stanley was going to have to start watching her husband's calorie intake if she wanted him to live past sixty. "Have Williams stick those reports on my desk before he leaves tonight."

"Will do," Rafe said with a nod, snapping instantly back into work mode and then glancing at his watch. Five thirty. Just enough time to swing by and pick up some beer and make it to Shane and Cat's for dinner. "I'm leaving now, but I have a call scheduled with him at eight o'clock tonight when he gets back from those witness interviews."

There had been a brutal assault on an elderly woman at a convenience store the morning before, and his partner was finishing up with the last few witnesses while he followed up with some telephone leads that had come in. So far, they didn't have much, but he was confident that Williams would manage to get some good info from a witness who claimed she was looking out her window when the attacker was fleeing the scene.

Until then, he'd eat a juicy burger with some friends. The only way to keep from burning out at this job was to make sure to temper the bad with the really good, and his life was pretty good. He had a satisfying job, and a few buddies he could count on. He didn't need or want the complication of a woman full time.

So when it came time to let Courtney go...wait, did they have two more scenes or one? He didn't know whether last night counted or not. There was no precedent to look to for the answer. Sex had been a planned activity for so long, there had never been any question. That spontaneous coupling, born from her need for comfort and his need to provide it, and reassure himself that she was all right? That she was there and unhurt and alive? It cheapened it to call it a scene.

He whipped off a quick text back to the group, got his shit together, and headed out into the lingering sunshine. Perfect evening for grilling. He slid behind the wheel of his car, stopped off for a six-pack, and then made the short trip to his friends' house.

He pulled up behind Courtney's car and put his own in

park, wondering if she was going to be more spooked about the robbery or about what had happened between them afterward. He sat for another long minute, wondering if maybe he should reconsider going in, when a sharp rap on the window snagged his attention. He turned to see Shane standing outside the car.

"Cat said your car was making a knocking sound and you wanted me to take a look?"

He opened the driver's-side door and stepped onto the pavement as Shane peppered him with questions about manifolds and carburetors, but he was only half listening. The other half was busy watching Courtney through the kitchen window as she talked to Cat. Her face was animated and she was smiling. That was good. Maybe she wasn't freaked out after all. Maybe she'd taken him at his word when he told her she was safe and the odds of her getting robbed again were nil. And maybe she also realized that the deeper connection between them the night before had been nothing more than two people in an emotionally charged situation taking comfort in each other.

Yep, maybe it was better not to go looking for trouble where there was none.

...

"You must have been terrified," Lacey said, leaning over the cloth-covered picnic table to squeeze Courtney's hand.

"Of course she was," Cat snorted. "But my girl kept a level head, grabbed herself a knife, and got her ass out of there. You done good, kid. I'm so glad you're okay."

Courtney smiled and shrugged. "It helped that Rafe was on the phone. He kept me calm. Or as calm as I could possibly be in that circumstance. If the zombie apocalypse comes—"

"Ha! You mean when the zombie apocalypse comes," Cat

corrected, and she stood to refill everyone's iced tea glasses.

"Okay, when it does, I'll take Rafe in my survivor camp any day." She sent him a shy smile, still not sure how to act around him. He'd been especially quiet since he'd arrived, and she wondered if he was having second thoughts about last night or was just preoccupied with work stuff as he claimed.

"I appreciate that," he said, tipping his head in her direction, but not meeting her gaze. "And best believe I'll take the ER nurse on my team in a heartbeat. Now if we can just find someone who can hunt once the food supply is depleted, we'll be set."

"I don't want to toot my own horn, but everyone knows I can fish my ass off," Galen said from his designated spot at the grill. "I'm thinking if someone needs to get voted off, we need to consider losing the deadweight. Shane here can't even cook a decent steak."

"I was dealing with the meat just fine until you got here and took over. You and your sister are both too bossy for your own good. Not conducive to communal lifestyles," Shane said, ignoring his fiancée's indignant gasp. "And plus, you and Lacey have the baby coming in a couple weeks. You're going to be so focused on her, you won't be able to think rationally. I've seen it a hundred times. It's the curse of all new parents."

The playful ribbing continued around them and Lacey made her case for inclusion in the war against zombies as Cat rose and motioned for Courtney to follow. "Want to help me with the salad?"

Courtney grabbed the tall, sweating glass of tea and trailed behind her friend into the kitchen.

"What's the deal?" Cat asked softly, with a glance at the door to make sure no one had followed.

"What do you mean?" God, she was the worst liar. Her cheeks were on fire and she pressed the chilled glass to one. "Hot out there, huh?"

"Don't give me that shit," Cat said, and began rustling through the refrigerator. "Something is brewing here, and I want to know what it is."

"I'm not sure," Courtney said cautiously. "We've had two of our scenes so far...well, maybe three?"

"You mean you don't know?" Cat threw an astonished look over her shoulder before rising, closing the refrigerator door with a hitch of her hip. "If that's the case, then he's definitely doing something wrong."

"No, it's not that. We, uh, slept together on three separate occasions but one of them was last night. After the break-in. It wasn't what I'd call a scene, but..."

"Seriously?" Cat asked, her face a mask of awe as the nimble hands opening a package of carrots for the salad slowed to a halt.

"Seriously. And it wasn't in the heat of the moment or anything. We just kind of woke up in the middle of the night and turned to each other." A warmth bloomed in her chest and she shook her head, bemused. "I'm sort of...nuts about him."

How crazy to hear those words coming out of her own mouth. A month ago, she would have bet a million dollars it would be years before she felt ready to dive into another relationship. But now, with Rafe? She was so filled with hope. Like anything was possible.

Her throat went tight and she took another sip of iced tea. Now she had to find out if he felt the same way. It sure seemed like he did. And if he wasn't ready to admit it yet, she had two more chances to convince him that they could be perfect together if only he was willing to take the chance.

Cat peppered her with questions as they chopped vegetables, and she filled her friend in on their night at the carnival as well.

"The Rafe I know would've begged off instantly," she

said. "He must really like your company, because he has hard and fast rules about dating outside of the scene life."

The words gave Courtney one more buoy of hope to cling to. By the time she finished telling Cat about Gil, and the Ferris wheel, she was more sure than ever that she and Rafe had a real shot of making things work. Chemistry aside, they genuinely liked each other's company and, with every passing minute, "like" was skidding perilously closer to "love."

For her, at least.

"Well, that sounds pretty frigging awesome. And I'd like to take the credit for escalating things between you guys again, but I actually did get called into work that night. High-profile client had a last-minute wedding dress emergency. In any case, I'll tell you this, you've never looked better," Cat said with an approving smile as she resumed her chopping while Courtney washed off some radishes at the wide porcelain sink. "You seem so confident and comfortable in your skin."

"Thanks." She wasn't sure she looked any different, but she sure felt different. Every new experience with Rafe lifted her up. That she could have the kind of sex that her body clearly craved with a man who also made her heart happy was something she had never even dreamed of.

"So are you going to tell him how you feel?" Cat picked up the cutting board and tipped its contents into a large wooden bowl. "Toss those in here whenever you're ready."

Courtney took the board and began to slice the radishes into neat discs. "I don't know," she said, tempering her excitement some. "I mean, I don't want to jump the gun."

"What do you think was the turning point?" Cat's gaze was filled with curiosity as she nibbled on a piece of celery. "Because I swear, you two were so stubborn. I thought I'd never see the day…"

She thought about that question for a long time before answering. "A lot of things. The way he was with me, so sexy and creative in bed, and then so fun and easy to be around the rest of the time."

She set the knife down and climbed onto one of the tall island stools, letting her legs swing while she talked. She glanced around to make sure everyone else was still outside chatting before she continued. "Before all this, I let things with Wes color my view of the world. He was controlling to the point of abuse and I never saw it coming."

Cat made to say something, but she held up a hand to stop her.

"I don't want you to feel bad for me. I know now that it wasn't my fault, and I'm happy to say that I've moved on. But it took two years to get here and I know Rafe, and even the scenes in a way, are responsible for that. I couldn't get my head around the idea that I could do those things with a person... let them say those things, and make demands on me sexually like that without turning into a doormat again. Doing them with someone who was no threat to me emotionally but who I trusted as a man was so freeing."

She tipped her head consideringly. "It hit me the night at the hotel." The epiphany she'd had excited her even now and she rested her elbows on the granite island. "Rafe is every bit as invested as I am. Every bit as vulnerable. I hold as much power over him as he does me. I'm trusting him to keep me safe even when he might be meting out a punishment, but the power he has is a direct result of my will. I offer that to him when we're doing a scene together, and he accepts and takes the reins from there, but it all starts with me. It makes me feel strong and sexy and beautiful."

And happy, she wanted to add, but Cat's eyes had clouded with worry.

"Makes sense to me, but don't underestimate how stubborn the man can be. If he did all the things you described, I'd put money on the fact that he's falling in love with you. He wouldn't have slept over at your house if he wasn't. But he's a tough nut," Cat said, bustling over to the double oven and taking out a pan of baked potatoes. "He's stuck to these ideas for five years now, and it's not easy to convince a man he's wrong sometimes. Especially not a man like Rafe."

"I know you're right. I might wait to say anything until we do the two other scenes. Give him a chance for his brain to catch up with the rest of him, maybe." At least, she hoped that was how it would go. "But before this is over, I'm going to tell him how I feel. That I'm crazy about him and that I think we could have something really special if he gave it a chance."

He'd done that for her. Helped her get the confidence and build the strength to risk her heart again. But it was still terrifying. Another trickle of nerves skittered through her and she pushed herself to her feet.

"Well, I'll be thrilled for you both," Cat said, gathering up the salad dressing and toppings. "And I'm sure the fact that he got the job done when no one else could doesn't hurt. If I were you, I'd put a ring on it, lickety-split."

Courtney chuckled, following behind with the large wooden bowl full of greens. She turned toward the door and froze in her steps when she saw Rafe standing there.

"Am I missing something funny, ladies?"

Courtney's laughter faded at the stark look on his face. Her heart stuttered and she risked a glance at Cat, who cleared her throat.

"I'm going to check on the burgers." She scurried out the back door onto the porch without a backward glance and Courtney's stomach pitched.

"What is she talking about, 'got the job done'?"

Chapter Thirteen

Rafe stood in the doorway between the dining room and kitchen, reeling. She was crazy about him? Euphoria came in almost hard enough to conquer the fear and denial. But not quite.

Courtney shifted restlessly under his gaze, and set the bowl she'd been holding on the granite island. "How long were you standing there?"

"Long enough. And I'm curious about the whole 'getting the job done' thing." That, of the things he'd heard, was the least of his concerns at the moment, but the last thing he wanted was to give her an opening to air her feelings about him right now. He had no fucking clue what he could say back, and needed some time to work it out.

She looked down at her hands, and twisted at the slim silver ring on her pinky. "I should have put it on the survey, I guess, but it wasn't really relevant and it's pretty embarrassing. Um, before you and I…that night after the reception? I'd never had an orgasm before."

He digested the information and tipped his head. It was still a stunning revelation. Not more stunning than the one banging around in his head like a ricocheting bullet, but still, a doozy. "With a man," he added and went back into the think tank, trying to determine how this affected their relationship, if at all. He didn't like the fact that she hadn't confided in him, but he understood why she hadn't.

"Why does everyone keep saying that?" She blew out an exasperated sigh. "No. Not with a man. I mean, at all."

He stared at her now. "Ever?"

She shook her head. "Never."

The first time she'd ever felt an orgasm in her life was with him. And the second time. And the third and fourth and the fifth. Fuck, no wonder she'd changed her tune so quickly.

One minute she wasn't sure she wanted a relationship with him and the next she was all about it, asking him to stay over. Not so astounding when he considered how everything progressed. He thought back to Lacey's bachelorette party when Courtney had grilled him about his sex life and how adamant she'd been that it was wrong for her. Then they'd had that spontaneous meet-up on the side of the road where it all started. He made her come and come hard, and all of a sudden her "nevers" and "no ways" became "probably nots" and "maybes".

Then after the first scene, she agreed to go to the carnival with him, opening herself even more. And after the other night at the hotel? He'd lost count of the times she'd screamed his name. Even last night…

He pushed last night out of his head with a brutal shove.

Boy, for a detective, he'd sure missed some major clues.

Or maybe you saw what you wanted to see.

"The form you sent me specifically asked if there was anything I should know about your sexual history, Courtney. I can't see how you thought this didn't qualify."

She looked so miserable, all the anger left him in a whoosh. Hell, she couldn't help it. Anyone who'd managed to get halfway through their twenties without coming was going to feel pretty warm and squishy about the first guy who did her right. Maybe she'd needed that extra push of fantasy and edge to throw her over, or maybe she'd finally let herself go enough to allow it to happen, but whatever the case, odds were good that this wasn't love at all. Near sick with relief and something else he refused to contemplate for too long, he met her gaze again, his path clear.

"Say something," she whispered miserably.

In spite of his clamoring emotions, he managed to keep his tone even. "That sucks for you. I'm sorry that it took this long to work it out."

"So that's it? You're not mad that I didn't tell you?"

"I wish you had. It's important to be totally honest and forthcoming when it comes to those surveys, but I'm not mad."

She nodded but still looked unsure. "Okay. Well, Lacey and Galen picked me up. Maybe you could give me a ride home after dinner and we can talk? The food's probably getting cold and Cat probably feels uncomfortable. We should go out and let her know everything's cool."

He crossed the room and held the door open, then followed her out. She brushed his arm with her fingertips and he wished he could give in to the urge to reassure her. To take her hand and give it a squeeze so she'd know everything was going to be all right. But he couldn't do that.

Because at this point? He was pretty sure nothing was going to be right at all.

Despite their agreement to talk, the ride home was almost silent. He hated making her feel bad and insecure. A dozen times, he'd opened his mouth to reassure her, but the fact was, he couldn't. Not if he was being honest.

"Williams got some new info on that convenience store

assault case. I have to meet him at the station to go over it. I can come in to check the house if you want, but I can't stay."

That much was true. His partner had called him after they'd finished dinner when Courtney was saying her goodbyes to Cat. He didn't add that there was no real reason they couldn't go over it on the telephone.

Because he needed to buy time. Time to decide what the fuck he was going to do. They had two more scenes together and he wasn't ready to give her up yet. He took a left onto her street and had almost convinced himself to turn around. To say fuck it and bring her back to his house like none of this had happened.

Then he remembered what it felt like to have his heart smashed into pieces. To love someone and lose them. Maybe Courtney loved him, and maybe, as he suspected, it was nothing more than her confusing lust with love. Either way, he wasn't willing to risk causing her more pain just so he could spend two more nights with her. That would make him a bigger bastard than her ex.

Now that she'd moved past her issues and gotten her confidence back she should get out there, meet people, find someone who could offer her something more than toe-curling orgasms.

When he allowed himself to consider the consequences of this decision—that by doing this, he was resigning himself to the fact that someday, maybe soon, there would be another guy curling her toes—he wanted to howl in fury.

Jealousy like he'd never felt before made his hands clench the wheel tighter until his knuckles turned white. His throat ached with the need to tell her that she was *his* woman. That the thought of another man touching her made him want to commit violence.

Instead, he pulled into her driveway and managed to grind out the words he'd been dreading.

"We need to talk."

...

A rush of blood hummed in her ears and she tried to shove back the rising tide of panic. Surely it couldn't be as ominous as it sounded. Not eighteen hours before, they'd been wrapped in each other's arms, his face lit with the same happiness she'd been feeling.

She pushed past the ache in her throat and nodded. "Okay, what about?"

It was going to be okay. It had to be.

"About us and the two remaining scenes."

Not okay. Her stomach flipped and she blinked back the tears pooling behind her lids. "Is this because of what you overheard at Cat's? I'm sorry I didn't tell you, but—"

"No. This is about me and my priorities. Things at work are crazy right now. Hell, I shouldn't have even left the precinct tonight. I'm in the middle of a case now and they've been coming back-to-back. I'm on track for a promotion and I've got to stay focused."

Could that really be it? But then why the sudden revelation? Still, a little ember of hope blazed in her heart.

"Well, when work calms down again, maybe?" She hated the pleading note that had crept into her voice but was helpless to stop it.

His jaw had clenched and he stared out the window for a long moment before answering. "I wouldn't count on that. But I had a great time with you," he continued, his tone impersonal but polite. "I'm impressed at how open-minded you were. I appreciate that more than you know."

Fury came in hot and fast, neatly replacing the despair.

Old Courtney might have let that sack of crap excuse stand, but new, improved Courtney wasn't about to let him off so easily. "You *appreciate* it?" She turned to glare at him now, her whole body trembling. "Well that's great, Rafe. Why don't you send me a fucking fruit basket along with a little thank-you note. 'Dear Courtney, I appreciate the copious amounts of ass. Warm regards, Detective Rafe Davenport.'"

"Don't be that way." He wouldn't look at her, instead keeping his gaze locked on her garage door. "Look, we spent some time together. We both enjoyed it. I think it's best if we leave it at that."

The anger drained away as quickly as it had come, and she shrank into her seat as utter despair settled over her. "The carnival, and last night…I know I wasn't alone in this. I know you felt it too."

He stayed stock-still and silent, his swift intake of breath the only indication that he'd heard her at all. "I don't understand why you're doing this," she whispered, one hand on the door handle, willing herself to open it before she embarrassed herself by begging.

"I hope someday you will."

Someday. Someday, long in the future, because they wouldn't be seeing each other anymore, whether his workload lightened or not.

She yanked the door open and got out of the car, tears blinding her.

"Courtney."

His voice was low now. Sad. She stopped but didn't face him, refusing to let him see her cry.

"Take care of yourself."

"Take *care* of yourself? That's it?"

The astonished look on Cat's face was enough to send a fresh crop of tears to Courtney's eyes. She nodded miserably and swiped a tissue over her face.

"Yeah, that's it."

"I don't get it," Cat said flatly. Her hands were balled

into fists at her side and her cheeks were ruddy with fury. She paced around the living room like a caged animal, back and forth over the beige carpet, looking as confused and helpless as Courtney felt. "I seriously want to strangle him right now."

They'd been going over and over it for the better part of an hour and operation "Cheer Courtney Up" had morphed into operation "Talk Cat out of Murder."

After Rafe dumped her a few nights before, she'd been in such a state of shock, she'd holed up like a wounded bear. She called in to work and took her three personal days, hunkered in with her Rosetta Stone and pint of Ben & Jerry's, which she was too nauseous to even eat. The only ray of light was that she was now food-fluent in Portuguese.

By the time Friday rolled around and an uninformed Cat called to see if she was going to meet them for happy hour, the dam had reached point break and her question was met with a racking sob. She'd been knocking at Courtney's door half an hour later.

"I can see him being a little put out that you didn't mention the orgasm thing," she conceded with a huff, "but breaking it off? Is that really what you think it was? It doesn't make any sense. If anything, he should be happy. Seems like something most guys would want chiseled onto their tombstone."

She came to an abrupt stop and wheeled around, throwing her arms out dramatically. "Here lies Rafe. Son... friend...hero...and purveyor of first-time orgasms."

Courtney only half listened as she listed to the side and rested her head on the velvety throw pillow, snuggling deeper into the couch cushions. If only she could sink all the way into them until they swallowed her like a cocoon. Then, someday when her heart stopped feeling like someone had put it through a meat grinder, she could crawl back out, whole again.

"I'd love to explain it to you," she said helplessly, "but I'm not even sure that was the reason. All he said was that he needed to prioritize. Think through some things, and that work had gotten really intense."

She'd known that for the lie it was when he wouldn't look at her as he said it. But then again, who was she to judge? She'd lied too. Maybe a lie of omission, but a lie nonetheless. Her stomach roiled as she recalled the expression on his face. Sad, yeah, but also resigned. Determined. There was nothing she was going to say that would change his mind, and she knew it.

That hadn't stopped her from trying.

Well, when work calms down again, maybe...

She shuddered at the memory.

Take care of yourself.

The words, so final, so generic but so telling, had been bouncing around in her brain for days.

She'd take care of herself because what other choice did she have? But she wondered if he had any clue how much he'd hurt her. As bad as she felt about her lie of omission, was it really so bad that it merited this, or was she missing his true motive entirely? She might never know because he hadn't seen fit to tell her.

Cat stayed with her the rest of the day, refusing to leave until Courtney had eaten a pint of wonton soup and a spring roll, and promised to get off the couch and take a walk that evening. After a tight hug punctuated with a warning that she'd be back on Sunday, she'd left Courtney alone with her thoughts.

Thoughts that were filled with Rafe. The way she felt when he touched her. The way he smelled. His smile. The way his eyes filled with that slow-burning heat when he looked at her.

Maybe she'd get past this and come out on the other side better for it in some way. Maybe she'd wallow for a while, pick herself up, and find someone new who made her feel the way he did. Maybe she'd be able to climb into bed at night, close her eyes and not see his face.

Someday.

Chapter Fourteen

Rafe pummeled the speed bag mercilessly, sweat stinging his eyes. It had been a month since he'd last seen her. Four weeks, three days and—he spared a glance at the clock on the dirty gym wall—one hour. Seemed like forever, and he was no more at ease with his decision than he had been the day he'd made it. In fact, if anything, he felt worse about it.

Last he heard, she wasn't doing so hot either. In this case, misery didn't love company. As much as it would've killed him to hear she'd landed another guy, he hated that she was hurting. Hated to think of her being sad.

Still not close enough to mental and physical exhaustion to call it quits, he'd just moved on to the heavy bag when a voice had him pausing, mid-jab.

"You want a sparring partner, or are you going to continue punishing Georgie's poor bags for the rest of the night?"

"Tell 'em, Galen," Georgie called from behind the desk at the entrance where he sat watching an old Frazier versus Ali fight on a black-and-white TV in the corner. "We were supposed to close at eight tonight."

Everyone who frequented "Georgie's oxing Gym"—the "B" fell off the sign twenty years ago—knew Georgie wasn't going home before midnight in any case. He'd always said the secret to his long, happy marriage was the fact that he and Ruth never spent more than three hours in the same room unless they were sleeping.

Rafe turned and eyed his friend. Galen and Lacey had been knee-deep in diapers, pink paint, and spit-up for the past two weeks. Oddly enough, his friend had never looked happier—he noted the bags under Galen's smiling eyes and a smile tugged at his lips—or more exhausted.

"Melina still getting her days and nights mixed up, huh?" Rafe asked, backing away from the bag, adjusting the tape on his hands.

Galen shrugged and chuckled. "I guess so. But I don't really give a shit. She's my little angel, and if I never slept again, I'd die a happy man."

Rafe couldn't deny it. The little butterball was pretty cute, and Lacey and Galen had taken to parenthood like they'd been made for it. Which made him wonder why, after weeks of sticking close to home with his new addition, his buddy had decided that swinging by Georgie's at eight thirty dressed in gym pants and a T-shirt stained with what Rafe could only hope was pureed peas seemed like a good idea.

"Cat told you I was here."

It wasn't a question. He'd run into Cat and Shane on his lunch hour and mentioned that he'd be stopping here before going to Sully's later tonight if they could slip away. Lately, alone had felt more alone than ever and the only time he felt halfway normal was when he was slammed at work or surrounded by people.

None of whom were Courtney.

Cat had tried to grill him when it first happened, but after years of friendship, she'd recognized a stone wall when she saw it. She'd been a little short with him for the first couple weeks, but once she realized this was taking as much of a toll on him as it was on Courtney, she'd relented. Now the band was back together, but short a member, and Cat and Lacey had started a side project—an all-girl trio—with Courtney.

They spent a lot of time helping with the new baby, and that was great for Lacey but also for Courtney. He was happy she had them. If she felt anything like he did, she surely needed friends around. But it still never ceased to make his guts hurt when Shane told him the girls were getting together. Silly to be jealous of two of the friends he loved most for getting to spend time with the girl he'd dumped.

What a dick.

Galen cleared his throat and raised a brow. "You want to do this or what?"

It had been a while since he'd sparred with Whalin' Galen Thomas, and that might be exactly what the doctor ordered. Who knew? Maybe the former heavyweight champ would land his patented haymaker and knock him out for a while. It would be the most rest he'd gotten in a month. Still, his mind was in more of a "seek and destroy mode" than one appropriate for sparring, and he tossed a nod to the training mitts in a box on the yellowing floor.

"I don't feel right hitting a man with baby puke on his shirt who probably spent the past month eating boxed mac and cheese. But you can be my hands if you want to."

It was a bad decision, and one that was going to cost him. If they'd sparred, at least the mouth guard would've kept him quiet for a while. Instead, he could see Galen gearing up for a speech as he donned the mitts.

"Look, man, I don't even know the whole story, but I can't imagine what could've happened that was so bad that it isn't even worth talking about trying to fix. I know you both well enough to know there was no cheating, no abuse, no drugs or stealing. So what then?" Galen held up his hands and nodded, signaling for Rafe to start throwing punches. "What's so bad that you can't man up and go to her?"

Rafe unleashed a jab-cross combo. *Thwap. Thwap.*

Galen pressed on when Rafe didn't answer. "Figure out a way to talk this through and see if there's another solution other than the two of you being alone and miserable. Unless you're hell-bent on acting like a stubborn ass."

Talking that kind of shit would've earned most guys a jab to the jaw, but he and Galen had been through enough together that he knew it for what it was. Some probably long-overdue tough love. That didn't stop him from blowing it out with a torrent of punches that had to have his boy's hands stinging even with the protective mitts.

"Nice," Galen nodded. "Still fast as hell. You should've gone pro. But don't try to distract me. Answer the fucking question."

Rafe ran a slick forearm across his damp face and stepped back. Might as well get it over with. It couldn't make things worse. "She neglected to disclose a couple important things."

"Like what?"

How much to tell him? Then again, he probably knew it all anyway. Secrets were hard to keep in their tight-knit group. He flickered a glance in Georgie's direction and said quietly, "Apparently, I was the first guy to get her off."

Galen nodded slowly. "Yeah, Lacey said that's the bullshit excuse you were trying to pedal. Maybe I'm being thick here, but I'm not seeing how that's a problem. And it damn sure isn't one to break up over. So why don't you tell me the real deal?"

His ice-blue eyes held a challenge and Rafe bit back a sigh. "You can't break up if you're not together. We had an agreement." He blew out a vicious breath and punched one of the mitts halfheartedly. "She thinks she's in love with me.

I heard her tell your sister."

"Talk me through what that little bit of info meant, to your mind." Galen shrugged a wide shoulder. "I can't promise I'm going to get it, or be able to offer any advice, but it might help to get it all off your chest."

"You know how she was at first. When Cat told her about my preferences. She pretty much called me out for it, and basically announced that she would never get down like that."

"And did that seem like a challenge to you?"

He made sure to think hard before he answered. "Maybe it did, but not enough to do anything about it. Not worth the damage. It was one of those 'Man, I'd love to spend some of my nights with those legs wrapped around me changing her mind,' but nothing more than that. And then we were at your wedding, and the garter thing…"

His mouth went dry as he recalled that night. The way her needs had called to his. The way her skin had felt under his fingers. "I got wrapped up in it. In her. We hooked up after the reception and it was…" He trailed off, torn between not wanting to share what had been such a deeply intimate moment and wanting to make Galen understand the magnitude of their chemistry. He settled for simple. "Man, it was fucking good."

Galen's curt nod told him he'd rogered that, loud and clear.

"After that, we were off to the races. I should've seen it coming. That we were getting in too deep. Maybe I did, but I didn't want to face it. It wasn't just the scenes. We talked in a way I haven't talked with a woman in…" He trailed off, letting his buddy fill in the blank.

Galen yanked off the mitts, looking thoughtful. Another minute went by and Rafe had about given up on a response when he finally looked back at him.

"You're a fucking idiot."

He blinked at his friend and straightened. "What the hell is that supposed to mean?"

"You're going to lose out on the best woman you'll ever get because you're stubborn and too much of a chickenshit to take a chance. That makes you a class-A idiot in my book."

"You're assuming that what she thinks she feels is real. Could be nothing more than the fact that I was the first guy she ever had a satisfying sexual relationship with."

"She's changed. You can see it in her. She's so confident and sure of herself, even now, being heartsick over you. She got her dick of a boss at work fired for mistreating the staff, she's been going toe-to-toe with Cat. Like she knows who she is and what she wants. I hate to say it, but…"

Galen's voice was sympathetic, and Rafe braced himself for the coming blow.

"You were a big part of that. You helped her get past the shit with her ex. Telling her how she needs to listen to her instincts, and how she's smart and strong and needs to trust herself. And then she does, and whether you want to admit it or not, falls in love with you. Then you turn around, dump her, and act like her feelings can't be trusted. Sounds like kind of a dick move to me. At least be honest with yourself. You're crazy about her too, and are too scared to admit it."

Damn. Galen always had a good right hook. Rafe glared at him, but the anger was surface only. He didn't answer, lost in thought, and a minute later Galen interrupted his thoughts.

"I gotta get back to Lacey and the baby, but think about what I said at least, would you?"

Rafe gave his friend a noncommittal grunt, but Galen didn't have to worry. Rafe was fairly certain he'd be able to think of nothing else for the foreseeable future.

He moved back toward the heavy bag and took a swing. Whatever his friend said, he knew one thing for sure. If he put his heart on the line and Courtney broke it, it would obliterate him. Maybe even worse than Monica's death had. He'd loved her the way a boy did his first love, and the guilt for what he'd accepted as his role in her death had compounded that heartbreak. But what he felt for Courtney was different. Complex. Deep. He could see a future with a woman like her. A life. It sparkled on the horizon like an untouchable star.

It took another forty-five minutes before he punched himself out, because he was hardheaded like that, but eventually, it became clear as crystal.

Galen was right. After all his big talk to Courtney after the break in, he was still letting fear control him, resigning himself to a life alone…a life without her so he never had to risk heartache again. But every day since he'd left her had been torture.

He finally got it.

Now, when he'd hurt Courtney so badly he wasn't sure she'd ever forgive him.

Now, when he'd failed her by convincing her to trust in herself and then walking away when she did.

Now, when it was probably too late to fix it.

But that wasn't going to stop him from trying.

He tapped out a quick text on his phone, waved to Georgie, and headed for the door.

"Go get 'er, kid."

...

"If you think I'm getting on that, you're even crazier than you look," Courtney said, eyeing the mechanical bull like it was on fire.

"It's perfectly safe," Cat said with a wave of her pen. "And if not"—she held the sheet of paper in her hand with her signature at the bottom aloft—"the waiver says you're entitled to up to ten thousand dollars in the event of sudden death or dismemberment."

"Oh, well that's different then. Sign me up."

Cat narrowed her eyes, studying Courtney's face. "That's sarcasm, yes? So you're saying you still don't want to do this?"

Courtney sighed and nodded. "That's exactly what I'm saying."

She glanced around the spacious room decked out in cow skulls, lassos, and saddles and asked herself for the tenth time since they arrived why she'd agreed to this. Country line dancing was so not her thing.

It wasn't Cat's either, but riding a mechanical bull had been on her bucket list, and after her ill-fated attempt at it a few years back—which had resulted in at least one broken bone—she'd been champing at the bit to take another crack at it. That was so like Cat. Taking the proverbial "falling off a horse and getting back on" sentiment to a whole other level.

"That's fine. We don't even have to stay all night. We'll check out the band and have a drink while we wait for my turn. In the meantime, maybe you can dance with that cute guy who's been staring at you since we walked in before we go."

Courtney followed Cat's glance across the bar to a good-looking guy in a cowboy hat who grinned when she met his gaze. He tipped his hat and she nodded back before looking away.

Tall, dirty-blond hair from what she could see, and piercing blue eyes that were so unusual in color that they were clearly visible from twenty feet away. She should've been moved. But she wasn't.

"Seriously?" Cat asked, setting down the consent form and shaking her head in despair. "He looks like Brad Pitt in *Thelma & Louise* and nada? Man, you do have it bad." She rubbed Courtney's back sympathetically. "I was trying to get you out of the house, but if you're not ready for this, we can go to Giardello's, get a big cup of cocoa and a fat slice of death by chocolate, and hang if you want to. I can do this any time." She tipped her head toward the bull and they both looked just in time to see a slim brunette woman go flying off the back of it and land in a heap on the mat a few yards away.

"Damn." Cat whistled. "That had to hurt." Even after witnessing the carnage, she still leaned forward in her chair, practically bouncing with excitement when the emcee got up to announce the next rider's name.

Courtney shook her head and fiddled with the straw in her margarita. Far be it from her to get in the way of her friend crossing another item off her bucket list…and possibly maiming herself. "It's fine. I don't think it matters where I am. It's going to take time to get over this whole thing, but I appreciate you looking out for me."

There had only been seven brave souls on the list to ride El Diablo, and they'd already gone through three of them, so it would likely be an early night anyway.

"Hi there. Hope I'm not interrupting, but I'd love to buy you ladies a drink…"

Courtney looked up, a polite smile and words of regret already cued up, when Cat piped in.

"We'd love one! I'm Cat, this is Courtney." She held her hand out like a spokesmodel on a game show when a contestant had won a "newww carrr!"

"I'm Jack." He tipped his hat again and nodded. "Pleasure to meet you both."

Courtney swallowed a sigh, and resigned herself to a few minutes of obligatory small talk. Lucky for her, Jack was easy to talk to, and an hour later, she found herself actually having a nice time.

She wasn't ready or looking for romance, and she told him that right off the bat, but making new friends hadn't always come easy for her. Chatting with someone as warm and personable as Jack was enough to bring a creaky smile to her lips at a time when smiles were few and far between.

When he asked her to dance, she let herself be cajoled. To her immense relief, he didn't hold her too close or make it weird. Instead, he told her stories about the rodeo circuit, and the creaky smiles evolved into rusty chuckles.

As he whirled and turned her this way and that, her thoughts, as they did every few minutes without fail, drifted to Rafe. Maybe all that chemistry wasn't a good thing after all. What had all the sizzling heat coupled with wild, out-of-control emotions gotten her, anyway? Heartbreak. Maybe an easy-to-be-with guy like Jack was the way to go.

Way less risk.

Something deep inside her responded instinctively, *But way less reward*.

And that was the rub. Now that she'd tasted what it could be like when she felt connected to someone both physically and emotionally, she'd never settle for less, risk be damned.

If she could only stop thinking about Rafe, maybe she'd have a shot in hell of finding it again.

Chapter Fifteen

Rafe eyed the scene before him, uncharacteristically frozen with indecision. He couldn't do what he wanted to do, which was walk over, tell Cowboy Jim to get his hands off his girl, throw her over his shoulder, and carry her out of this place. Because that would be insane. But the alternative—just standing by and watching while this guy pawed all over her—was making his stomach ache.

He was still no closer to figuring out how to handle it when Cat sidled up to him.

"I'm guessing you're not here to do the Boot Scootin' Boogie?"

He shook his head, never taking his eyes off Courtney. God, she looked beautiful. Hair up in a knot the way he loved it, orange camisole making her skin glow like burnished gold, white cotton miniskirt swishing around her thighs as she moved. No wonder Cowboy Jim looked like he'd struck oil.

"Cat, I don't even know what that is," he said grimly.

She chuckled and gave his shoulder a squeeze. "It's a country line dance. I think. But either way, I'm glad you're here."

As much as he appreciated the support, he couldn't help but wonder if she was going to be the only one. Courtney didn't look miserable now. Maybe she already had one foot on the path to moving on, and expecting her to forget everything that had happened and trust that he wouldn't hurt her again was naive of him.

He flexed his jaw as Cowboy Jim dipped his girl. Maybe this was a train wreck in the making, but he'd never forgive himself if he didn't at least try.

"Good luck," Cat called after him.

He strode onto the dance floor, singular purpose making it easy to cut through the crowd. By the time he reached Courtney and her dance partner, a strange calm had overtaken him, and he was grateful for it because it gave him the wherewithal to manage a tight smile for Cowboy Jim instead of the introduction to his fist that felt so much more natural.

"Hey there, buddy. Mind if I talk to the lady for a minute?"

To his credit, the cowboy didn't respond right away. He looked to Courtney, whose eyes were wide with shock.

"I think that's up to the lady, friend."

Seconds ticked by, and his heart picked up a beat for every one of them.

"What are you doing here?" she whispered.

Jim released her and stepped back. "I'll be at the bar if you need me," he said quietly as the song came to a close.

Courtney nodded but didn't take her eyes from Rafe. They were so filled with hurt it was enough to obliterate even the tiniest bit of confidence he'd had in this plan. Hadn't he done enough damage?

"Why did you come?" she asked again, her bottom lip trembling.

He stared at her and shook his head slowly. *Keep it*

simple. "Isn't it obvious, Courtney? I came for you."

"Obvious?" Her brows rose along with her voice. "You dumped me with nothing but some lame-ass explanation and drove off without a backward glance. Now you decide to show up more than a month later out of the blue? Maybe I'm missing something, but no. It's not obvious. What's changed, Rafe? Work let up some so you thought you could try to get another piece?"

He winced and drew back but didn't try to defend himself against that. He deserved it, and more. Maybe keeping it simple was off base. "Listen, can we go talk somewhere?"

"No." She crossed her arms over her chest and glared at him. "I'm here with my friend, and I'm not going to be one of those women who drop everything every time a man comes knocking. You want to talk, talk here, or call me and make an appointment like a regular person. You lost the right to pop up and expect my undivided attention when you walked away from us."

She stalked off the dance floor and past a sheepish Cat, through a door labeled BUCKARETTES.

As he followed that same path, Cat called out to him. "You know that's the ladies' room, right?"

He sure as hell did, and he could not give one single shit. He'd let Courtney go once out of sheer stupidity, and he wasn't about to make the same mistake again. As the door slammed behind her, he found himself wondering how he'd ever thought she wasn't strong enough to know her own mind. Strong enough to decide for herself whether or not what she was feeling was more than sexual attraction.

He barreled through the door behind her, and she wheeled on him.

"Are you serious right now?" Her hazel eyes blazed with fire as she stared up at him.

"Give me five minutes of your time, and then I'll leave

you alone."

She surveyed the pink room consideringly and seemed ready to deny him, but then she locked eyes with him and hers went soft. It was a split second, but it was enough.

"Please. I'm begging you."

She bit her lip and gave him a curt nod. "Three minutes."

He did a quick assessment of the things he needed to say and led with the most important. The unvarnished truth that he'd barely gotten a handle on himself.

"I'm fucking crazy about you, too."

She blinked as her cheeks went pink, but she said nothing. That was better than punching him in the nuts, so he pressed on.

"The past month has been hell and every single day was a battle to keep myself from picking up the phone and telling you that I changed my mind. That I was a chicken for burying my head in the sand and not giving us a chance. Begging you to forgive me. Feeling so desperate to be with you that at points, it didn't matter whether your feelings were real or not, as long as I had you in my life." He reached out and cupped her soft cheek. "But it does matter and—"

She pulled away, the softness in her eyes going hard again. "What do you mean, if my feelings were real?" The question was sharp enough to draw blood, and he flinched.

"I thought things were confusing between us. That maybe, because we started off with sex as the core of our relationship and then you had your first orgasm, what you were feeling was something more like…" He trailed off, knowing that, no matter how he said it, it was going to sound shitty.

She saved him the trouble as her face lit with dawning understanding. "You thought it was gratitude?" Her voice was shrill with shock. "I was so grateful that you'd waved your magic wand"—she jabbed a thumb toward his dick—"and abracadabra'ed up some orgasms that I decided you were my one and only?"

The door swung open, and a young woman in a waitress uniform stood at the entrance, mouth agape. "I'm sooo sorry." Clearly she'd heard enough to be mortified and backed slowly from the room. "Y'all continue on. I'll be back in a few."

Courtney didn't even glance her way. Her chest rose and fell furiously and her foot tapped a Latin beat on the tile.

"Is that what you honestly thought?"

It sounded so dumb when she said it, but that was *exactly* what he'd thought. "I care about you. I've never felt this way about a woman before, and I wasn't thinking straight either. I was trying to protect myself, and in some twisted way, protect you too."

She stopped tapping, and the fury in her eyes dimmed.

"I guess part of me was afraid if I admitted how I felt about you, I'd be vulnerable again." He shifted closer to her and muttered. "Having you for real and then losing you? I could stand anything but that."

...

Butterflies exploded into action in her belly. His face was so sincere, so full of genuine regret, it was hard to maintain her fury. Especially when all it would take was one act of forgiveness and two steps to put her in his arms again.

But she couldn't do that. Not yet. He'd said what he'd needed to say and now it was her turn.

"That's the thing, Rafe. I *had* clarity." She shook her head and swiped back the tears that came. "You didn't even give me a chance to tell you how I felt. To tell you what *I* wanted. We could have worked this out if you'd trusted in me enough to tell me the truth about what was bothering you."

His face fell and her heart fell right along with it. "So you're saying we can't work it out now."

Funny how she hadn't been sure of the answer to that question until this very moment. The moment she realized that the thought of going back to being without him was a million times worse than taking the risk of being with him.

"Courtney?"

She shrugged. "I don't know what to say. If you can't talk to me and tell me how you're feeling, how can we ever work through anything?"

He stepped toward her and took her hand. "You're right. And if you give me another chance, I'd never do that again." His voice rang with such honesty, her pulse gave a little leap of hope.

Now was the time for caution, though. She wasn't sure she could go through losing him again. "Why should I believe that?"

Rafe pursed his lip and laced his fingers with hers. "Because I've regretted my decision since the day I walked away. And because I'm in love with you, and I will do anything it takes to earn your love again in return."

He *loved* her.

The words crept into her soul and wrapped around her heart like an embrace.

"You know, I'm not the expert, but I'm pretty sure if you're going to beg, you should be on your knees," she murmured softly.

He gazed down at her, his eyes going from bleak to hopeful. "That's fair." He dropped to his knees on the tile floor without hesitation. "So I'm begging for real now. We can start from scratch if that's what you need. I can take you to dinner one night, we can see a movie. Act like we just met. Take it slow." He tugged a folded sheaf of papers from his pocket and held them out to her. She took them with a shaking hand and peered down to read.

"A contract?"

He nodded. "To negotiate a new agreement. Make changes, add, delete. Whatever you want to do, do it. I'll sign. Because I trust that you know yourself and care about me enough to make it fair and good for both of us, if you'll have me."

"This says you're going to learn Greek. And Spanish? Oh, and the end date portion is blank," she murmured, the words barely making it past her achy throat as she clenched the paper tightly.

"That's right." His gaze was nailed to hers and she could feel the tension rolling off him. "Because I don't ever want to let you go. I want to retire with you and travel the world and speak bad French with you. Tell me you're in, Court. I dare you."

She considered letting him sweat a little, but couldn't bear to be away from him for another second. She closed the distance between them, dropping low in front of him. "We could take it slow like you said, I guess…" She let a hand drift down his chest to his abdomen. "Or we could act like we just met and then take it fast."

His eyes blazed as he caught her meaning and the warmth that had been blossoming in her chest went white hot.

"I won't blow it this time. I swear," he murmured, leaning in to press his lips to hers, tugging her to her feet along with him until they were standing, plastered against each other. She let herself get swept away in the moment, in the man, until a knock at the door sounded.

"Can I come in yet? I'm sorry but I really gotta go."

They broke apart laughing and she grabbed his hand, dragging him toward the exit. "We've got to get out there and watch our friend ride a bull," she said, smiling so hard it hurt her cheeks. "And then…"

"And then," he said, yanking her to a stop so he could nip her ear, "we'll see about setting up a ride of our own."

Epilogue

Courtney glanced down at her cell for the third time in an hour. Nine forty-five. His note had specifically said nine thirty and not to be late. She blew out a sigh and snagged a breadstick from the basket on the table. When her phone vibrated a second later, she grabbed it from the crisp peach linen cloth and peered down at the screen to see a text message.

Good girl. Five points for punctuality and another ten for that sexy as fuck dress. Now put the breadstick down and slide your hand under the table and between your legs for me, love.

She glanced around wildly, searching the surrounding tables for Rafe. It was a Saturday night, and the place was jammed. Chatter filled the room, and a musical duo played some classic R&B hits in the corner. She scanned the area twice but saw no sign of her man.

Her phone buzzed again.

Stop stalling and do what I told you, or prepare to

face the consequences.

She frowned, still wondering where he was hiding, but in spite of her confusion, her body was already warming to his demands.

With a surreptitious glance around to make sure no one was looking her way, she set down her breadstick, brushed the crumbs off on her napkin, and slipped her hand under the tablecloth to settle between her thighs. She'd worn a short dress at his request, and was thankful for it now as she didn't have to wriggle or move to make room. With a subtle shift of her hips, she spread her legs wide enough to accommodate her fingers and laid them over her quickly heating flesh.

Rub that clit for me now.

Her nipples went tight beneath the lacy bodice of her tank dress and she let out a low hiss. After six months together she should be used to it. The out-of-control, wild lust he inspired. The inventive, "close to the edge but never over it" scenarios he came up with. The man was lethal, and every day was an adventure. She'd never been happier.

For every ten seconds you make me wait, add another lash to your next flogging.

Worst. Warning. Ever. Already, she was wriggling her ass against the seat in anticipation. Still, his texts were making her hotter by the second and suddenly not only did she want to please him, she also wanted to ease the pressure building between her legs at a breakneck speed.

Keeping a watchful eye, thankful he'd booked a table in the corner, she gave in to the need, rubbing the tight bundle of nerves in slow circles. Pinching her bottom lip between her teeth, she held back a groan at the contact.

Could he see her still? Did he know she'd started? A

shiver ran through her, and she increased the pressure, letting out an involuntary gasp as her fingertips grew slick.

Beautiful. The waiter is bringing over a glass of merlot for you. I want you to keep touching yourself when he does. Don't stop. I'll know if you do, and you'll be punished. Once you've ordered your food and he leaves, drink your wine. All of it, fast. Nod if you understand.

She wet her lips and nodded, still scanning the room for some sign of him. Right then, her waiter rounded the corner, and she froze. How was she going to pull this off?

"Your wine, miss. From the gentleman at the bar." He set the goblet filled with ruby liquid on the table and tugged a white notepad from his apron with a flourish. "Are you ready to order?"

She couldn't help but lean forward to peer into the bar, and sure enough, there he was. Rafe, dressed in a pair of her favorite jeans that clung to all his best parts. His gaze locked with hers and the blatant need in his eyes gave her an extra dose of courage.

She cleared her throat and offered a smile at the server, all the while making figure eights over the aching flesh between her thighs. He read the specials as her legs quaked, her heart pounded, her pulse skittered. She felt the heat of Rafe's stare the whole time and she played to him, making sure to meet his eyes every few seconds for a moment.

"What do you recommend?" she managed, after he'd completed his spiel.

"The rack of lamb is delicious," he said with a smile.

Her phone buzzed and she glanced down quickly.

Two fingers. Slide them deep.

She deleted the text with one hand and followed Rafe's instructions with the other, tucking her index and middle fingers into her now pulsing channel.

"The lamb's fine," she managed, albeit in a choked voice. He asked a question about salad which she must have answered to his satisfaction because a second later, he was gone and she was two minutes from coming.

Drink.

A fine sheen of sweat beaded on her upper lip and suddenly drinking seemed like a great idea. If he made her get through this whole meal and the ride home without coming, she was going to kill him.

She gulped the wine down until the glass was empty and then wiped her mouth delicately with her napkin as she worked herself closer and closer to the edge. Her phone vibrated again and she snatched it up.

Stop what you're doing and head toward the restroom, but continue past it to the green door. When you get there, open it and walk through.

She looked up to find his former stool empty, and her pulse careened wildly. After straightening her dress, she stood, picked up her purse, and crossed the room. The wine had gone straight to her head, and the slightly tipsy feeling only amplified her excitement.

When she reached the green door, she took a quick look around and swung it open, adrenaline coursing through her as she waited for an alarm to sound or for someone to come running out and reprimand her.

No one came and no alarm sounded.

She stepped into the cold, dark alleyway, her body aflame with anticipation in spite of the temperature. When two big, rough hands closed over her bare shoulders and shoved her against the wall, she should've been terrified. Instead, she was elated.

"You're so fucking sexy," he growled against her ear. The warm, earthy scent of his familiar cologne made her senses sing almost as much as the feeling of him grinding against her, putting the pressure right where she needed it.

He swooped down, slanting his lips over hers, and she whimpered into his mouth, already at point break. Hooking one stiletto-capped leg around his hip, she lined up her overheated core with his bulging erection, tearing her mouth away when he flexed hard in a sinuous rub.

"God, Rafe, please don't make me wait."

His voice was stark with want. "Ten minutes, remember Court?" he ground out, yanking at his jeans until his cock sprang free. "I wanted ten minutes in an alley with you and made a promise that kept me awake some nights. Tonight I'm going to make good. You'll be back inside in time to enjoy your lamb."

Joy bubbled like champagne inside her. He remembered how they'd begun, took the time to create a scene from their history. Because he loved her. She started to laugh, but her laughter was cut short as the broad, swollen head of his cock butted against her heat.

"That's my girl," he whispered softly, his breath a cloud of white in the icy night air. He pinned her more fully against the unyielding brick and swung her other leg up until she was able to lock her ankles around his waist. The move coupled with a swivel of his hips sent him deep and her vision went hazy.

"Y-you feel so good." And he did. It was sublime, how well they fit. How his body—like Rafe himself—pushed her to the limits, knowing right when to stop. *Just don't stop now*, she wanted to scream as he shifted. He cupped her ass in both hands, using the leverage to work her over his cock in long, hard strokes.

She flexed her thighs around him tighter and struggled to keep the wave from sucking her under before it was time. "I'm going to come already. Tell me I can, babe, please." She didn't care that she was begging, so long as it worked. There were nights that he made her hold out for longer than she ever thought she could, but if tonight was one of them, she would surely die.

"Fuck yeah," he bit out through clenched teeth.

His movements became frantic. The scrape of the gritty, cold brick abrading her ass, the slide of his swollen cock filling her to bursting, the knowing grip of the man she loved, it was all too much, and she hurtled toward release.

He kissed her then, a mash of lips and teeth and tongue, and she cried out into his mouth as she splintered into a million pieces. He followed a second later, and they shuddered together, their shared breath coming in gasps.

"That…" He swallowed hard and let out a short laugh, before pressing a kiss to her nose. "That was something right there, Nurse DeLollis."

She chuckled and let her legs go limp. "You got that right, Detective Davenport."

He set her down and glanced down at his watch. "With four minutes to spare." He held up a hand for a high five and she obliged him. He gripped her wrist at the last second and held her gaze, the smile sliding from his face. "You're the best thing that's ever happened to me, do you know that, Court?"

She nodded, but her cheeks burned with delight anyway. "I'm glad you think so because I love you like crazy."

"That's real good. Perfect, in fact." He cupped her chin in his hand and the grin was back as if by magic. "Now go eat your lamb and make it snappy. It just occurred to me that I live with a nurse, and we've never played doctor."

She straightened her clothes and headed back into the

restaurant, a secret smile tugging at her lips. He might not realize it, but he'd played doctor a long time ago, when he'd managed to heal her broken heart.

"Yes, sir," she said with a curt nod. "Now if we can only find a nurse's uniform that will fit you."

About the Author

USA TODAY bestselling author Christine Bell is one half of the happiest couple in the world. She doesn't like clowns or bugs (except ladybugs, on account of their cute outfits), but loves movies, football, and playing Texas Hold 'Em. Writing is her passion, but if she had to pick another occupation, she'd be a wizard. She loves writing fun, sexy contemporary romances, but also hopes to one day publish something her dad can read without wanting to dig his eyes out with rusty spoons.

Christine can be found at:
Website
Twitter
Facebook

Discover the Dare Me series…

DOWN FOR THE COUNT

DOWN AND DIRTY

DOWN THE AISLE

Also by Christine Bell

DIRTY TRICK

DIRTY DEAL

WIFE FOR HIRE

GUARDIAN FOR HIRE

REFORMING THE ROCK STAR

CONNED

Enjoy more heat from Entangled...

WET AND RECKLESS
a Private Pleasures novel by Samanthe Beck

Aspiring singer/songwriter Roxy Goodhart's latest mistake is a doozy, involving a lying ex-manager, a dire lack of cash, and a teensy bit of grand larceny. Landing in the long, strong, entirely too tempting arms of the law is no way to keep a low profile. Taking an apartment puts her under orderly West Donovan and in his path every day. Testing his impressive reserve is beyond reckless, but she'd love to test it...all...night...long.

LIKE A BOSS
an Accidentally Viral novel by Anne Harper

As if it wasn't bad enough that her long-term boyfriend dumped her, Nell Bennett goes viral online for ranting in a restaurant about her perpetually single status. Thankfully a kind and attractive stranger offers to share his table with her...and their sizzling banter leads to a surprising kiss before they part ways. Now her tiny hometown of Arbor Bay is buzzing over their latest Internet celebrity, but Nell's no stranger to attention. Still, even she never expected to show up to work only to discover her brand-new boss is a very familiar face...

FOLLOW ME UNDER
a Follow Me novel by Helen Hardt

Dating Boston's billionaire bachelor has opened up a new world for Skye Manning. So why does she feel like she's losing herself? Braden Black never meant to fall for Skye, and he still tries to resist a relationship he knows he's not wired for. But not only has Skye awoken something inside him—he's stirring something dark and forbidden inside his Cinderella. Something even he can't control...

Made in United States
Troutdale, OR
04/27/2025